One

As the sharp left-hand corner came up, Lee Parnaby shifted a trifle nervously in the seat of his bike but didn't reduce the revs. This time, he was determined to take it at maximum speed to set himself up for the downhill jump. His green-and-silver machine, freshly tuned, was responding beautifully. It had, he felt, never been better. So, this time, it was his own nerve, not the bike's performance, that was being put to the test.

Delicately his fingers played the throttle as he positioned the bike for the turn. Then, tilting, stabbing down with his left foot, trailing it over the loose earth, he was through the angle and racing towards the most fearsome hazard on the Skalbrooke Schoolboy Motorcycle Club's circuit. It was an approach he'd made hundreds of times in the past couple of years. But never had he approached it at the speed he was doing now.

Suddenly, his mouth went utterly dry. His

5

tongue felt huge. After all, the last time he'd attempted a very fast downhill jump he'd crashed. And that was only ten minutes ago, as he couldn't help remembering. His weight, he'd since worked out, had been in the wrong place on landing. He'd been too far forward and the front wheel came down first, spilling him helplessly across the track. Amazingly, though, he'd done no damage to himself or the bike. Perhaps, that time, he'd just been lucky. . . .

Instinctively now, he re-distributed his weight towards the rear. The trees clutching the hillside below seemed to tilt at him as the ground fell away. On the rim of the hill, it would disappear completely beneath him. His fingers tightened their grip.

He went into the take-off full-bore, hauling back on the handle-bars with all his strength as if trying to drag the whole bike into his chest. Like an Olympic downhill ski-jumper, he was shooting out into the unknown, striving desperately to make the perfect, balanced landing necessary to stay in the competition. To land – and still be running; that's what mattered.

The thump as the rear wheel banged down on unyielding stone jarred his entire body. Momentarily, the machine wavered. Then, closing down the throttle in order to brake effectively, he had control again. He'd done it!

MICHAEL HARDCASTLE

Fast from the Gate

MAMMOTH

Also by Michael Hardcastle

Motocross Stories
The Green Machine
Roar to Victory
Tiger of the Track

Football Stories
Away From Home
Free Kick
Half a Team
Mascot
Soccer Special
The Team That Wouldn't Give In
United!

Riding Stories
The Saturday Horse
The Switch Horse
Winning Rider

Caught Out   (A Cricket Story)
Rival Games   (An Athletics Story)
The Shooters   (A Netball Story)

Illustrated by Patrice Aitken

First published in Great Britain 1983
by Methuen Children's Books Ltd
Magnet paperback edition published 1984
Published 1990 by Mammoth
an imprint of Mandarin Paperbacks
Michelin House, 81 Fulham Road, London SW3 6RB
Reprinted 1992
Mandarin is an imprint of the Octopus Publishing Group,
a division of Reed International Books Ltd
Text copyright © 1983 Michael Hardcastle
Illustrations copyright © 1983 Patrice Aitken
ISBN 0 7497 0443 8
A CIP catalogue record for this title
is available from the British Library

Printed in Great Britain
by Cox & Wyman Ltd, Reading, Berkshire

Lee yelled his success to the world, though no one actually heard him. Like quicksilver, he flowed into the next bend; and the line he took was the perfect racing line. He hadn't had to think about it. His instincts as a scrambles rider had worked it out for him like a computer.

It was the fourth time in no more than about twenty minutes that he'd tackled that jump at high speed – and the first time he'd brought it off successfully. He wouldn't claim he'd mastered it but at least he knew he was coping with it in the right way. Never again would it terrify him, however fast he was going on take-off.

A downhill jump, Lee decided as he turned off the track to take a short cut back to the paddock area, was simply there to encourage a *winning* rider to win more convincingly.

He stood on the footrests, guiding the bike with infinite caution round a couple of bushes like a trials rider, and then increased the pace to bounce happily over a ribbed section to rejoin the main circuit. All evening he'd been refining his skills as a scrambler, working systematically in areas where he knew there was room for improvement. It was the start of a new season and Lee was determined to build on his success of the previous year. He'd won Intermediate races for the first time and established himself as one of the leading riders in his age-group in the Club. His ambitions were increasing all the time. At present, his chief aim was to gain selection for Skalbrooke's team for the Inter-Club races over the next few months.

The almost deserted paddock area was in sight when Lee spotted his cousin, Joanne Wragby, heading towards him. With her shoulder-length auburn hair streaming behind her and wearing her favourite rainbow-patterned sweater, she wasn't hard to recognise even from a distance. She wasn't so much running as making a connected series of successive long-jumps. Lee, who was exceedingly fond of his cousin, even though he didn't always show it, grinned behind his visor. The manner of Joanne's progress seemed to reflect her enthusiasms. It was her father, Ken Wragby, who'd introduced Lee and his brother Darren to motocross and provided them with their first bikes. He'd assumed that Joanne, because she was a girl, wouldn't be the slightest bit interested in such mechanised sport. That was quite wrong. Joanne, having grown up with bikes, had developed a great interest in them. Once she'd proved to her father that she was a perfectly capable rider, too, he'd promised her a bike of her own. She was due to receive it on her next birthday in July.

'Well, how did it go?' she demanded to know as Lee did a deliberately spectacular skid and came to a halt beside her. 'I hope you weren't doing all this show-off stuff out there on the track?'

'Nobody out there to see it – I hope. To be honest, I came off a couple of times when I really powered into that downhill jump. Then the first time I stayed on board after the jump I nearly came off again after landing because the bike was weaving about like a mad horse! I think I didn't come down early enough on the back wheel.'

'But you got it right in the end, Lee?'

'Er, just about, I think. Took off like a rocket – and kept going like a champion hare.'

'You've pinched that description from my essay for the school magazine!' she retorted accusingly. 'But it wasn't a rocket – that's too obvious. It was an intergalactic missile.'

'Couldn't pronounce that!' Lee confessed, trying not to laugh. 'Anyway, it felt terrific when I did it the last time so that must mean it works. I reckon even the Mad Motocrosser himself couldn't have done better – *and* stayed upright on two wheels.'

'Ah, talking of Greg Shearsmith, I think we'd better hurry up, Lee. He and his Dad want to get off home. They sent me out to see if you were on the way back.'

'O.K. Want to hop up on the back for a free ride to the pits?'

'What do you think I came all this way for?'

With alacrity she slid on to the long saddle and then clasped her hands behind her back instead of putting her arms round the driver. Lee, as he'd

9

once told her, felt 'hemmed in' when anybody did that.

By now the light on this evening of early spring was fading quickly, as mist from the estuary swirled inland. Because he'd been so absorbed by his private practice session Lee hadn't realised how late it was. He hoped Harry Shearsmith, Greg's father, wasn't going to complain that Lee had delayed their departure. In recent weeks Lee had come to rely heavily on Mr Shearsmith's generosity in transporting him and his bike to and from the Skalbrooke Club's circuits. Lee's father was in the Merchant Navy and thus mostly away from home.

Mr Shearsmith already had the engine of his expensive new minibus running when Lee, having accelerated over the final stretch and through the paddock area, reached the car park. He seemed calm enough but Greg was plainly angry even before he said a word.

'Did you fall off and knock yourself out?' he asked scathingly. 'We've been waiting ages for you, Lee. And I *told* you I wanted to get home in time to see that "Profile of a Boxer" programme. Probably miss half of it by the time we get there *now*.'

'Sorry,' Lee mumbled, feeling genuinely contrite. 'I just wasn't thinking about the time.'

Silently Mr Shearsmith propelled Lee's bike up the ramp and into the van. Carefully he secured it in the travelling frame alongside the black and gleaming Shearsmith Special, custom-built by himself. Greg's father was not only a very clever mechanic but a man with a talent for making money with all sorts of enterprises.

'Practice go well, did it son?' he asked Lee as he settled himself behind the wheel.

'Well, not bad in the end. I was trying to improve my, er, style on downhill jumps. I fell off a couple of times but I think I'd sorted things out by the time I packed it in.'

'I never think about changing *my* style for different bits of the course,' Greg announced from the front seat. 'Soon as I see daylight ahead of me I go flat out to win. Only way to ride a race, in my opinion.'

'So I'd noticed,' was Lee's quiet comment as he exchanged a knowing look with Joanne.

'Well, I've won as many scrambles as you, Lee Parnaby – and put up some of the fastest times on record,' Greg, whose hearing was acute, added.

Lee couldn't deny it. There were times when he couldn't help admiring Greg's fear-naught-and-stop-at-nothing approach to a motocross. Young Shearsmith really would go full speed into any danger spot without regard to the possible consequences. It took a certain degree of cold-blooded courage to do that. On the other hand, he certainly didn't care for Greg's sometimes totally ruthless attitude towards his fellow riders. It wasn't unknown for him to knock other competitors out of his way when he saw, or thought he saw, an opening. He'd caused several spills in the pack in his time and been suspended for reckless riding. Greg had a high opinion of his own skills but he never failed to mention how much he owed to his father's 'wizardry with the spanners,' as he put it. Without any doubt, the Shearsmith Special, with its novel spread-of-power exhaust system, really was a marvellous machine.

Lee himself was grateful to Mr Shearsmith, who had provided both transport and tuning services when Lee had needed them for a club meeting the previous season. That was really the start of his friendship – if that's what it was – with Greg. He had the impression that, for some unexplained reason, Mr Shearsmith rather liked him and wanted to help him whenever help was needed. Yet Lee believed that he himself was different in almost every way from Harry Shearsmith's own son.

Now it was Mr Shearsmith who deftly turned the conversation to the subject of the first round of the Inter-Club Championship. It was his view that the selectors on the Skalbrooke Committee would have to pick both Greg and Lee for the Intermediates' team. Lee tried to suppress a grin when he realised that Mr Shearsmith wasn't including his brother, Darren, among the leading candidates. But then, Darren hadn't made much progress in the past year.

'Come on, Dad, step on it!' Greg urged as the minibus hovered on the tail of a rather lumbering saloon. 'I don't want to miss any *more* of that programme! I want to see the way Charlie McQuade knocked out that giant Italian. In the preview they said there'd be a terrific slow-motion replay.'

'I'm doing my best, son. No point in taking risks on a narrow, winding road like this.'

'Look, Mr Shearsmith, you don't have to take us right to my house – I mean, I know it's a big detour for you,' Lee suggested. 'If you drop us at top end of Lingdale Village we can easily wheel the bike home from there. We can take the short cut through Terson's Fields and that new estate.'

Harry Shearsmith hesitated for a moment or two before he made any reply; and in that interval he shot a sideways glance at his son. Lee had been aware for some time that Mr Shearsmith gave in rather easily when Greg wanted something. So he had no doubt at all that Mr Shearsmith would take the opportunity to shorten his journey. Still, that was only fair, in Lee's opinion.

'Well, if you really don't mind, Lee,' was the predictable comment. 'Certainly it would help us.'

So, after steering a neat course to avoid some boisterous revellers spilling from the pavement outside The Dog and Partridge Inn, he pulled up on the broad parking area outside St Alban's, Lingdale's famous church-on-a-mound.

'Lucky for him I didn't knock one of those lads down,' remarked Mr Shearsmith, glancing back towards the pub as he unmoored Lee's motorcycle. 'He came so close he must have very nearly brushed against the van. Expect it's a party of young farmers celebrating something or other. It's their favourite pub.'

Lee took charge of the bike as soon as it touched the road and thanked him for his kindness.

'Sure you'll be all right on your own, then, Lee?' he asked anxiously if a trifle belatedly.

'Of course! In any case, I'm not on my own, am I? I told you, Joanne's staying with us this weekend while Uncle Ken and Aunt Sue are away in Paris. So she can do her share of pushing the old bike across the fields, can't you, Jo?'

'If you say so, Master,' she replied in a servile manner that made Mr Shearsmith laugh quite loudly.

'Right, then, we'll get off,' he said, slamming the door of the van. 'I'll pick you up at the usual time on Sunday for the club meeting. So long then – and take care.'

'You know, nobody would see us if we rode the bike across Terson's Fields,' Lee suggested. 'It'll be a real slog pushing it all the way. *And* it'll take ages.'

14

'Well, it's your own fault, Lee,' Jo pointed out. 'You were the keen one who told him to drop us off a thousand miles from home. You deserve to suffer. But you'll suffer a lot more if the police spot you riding a scrambles bike in the dark on public land. They'd probably never let you ride again, anywhere.'

Lee was just steering the bike into a narrow passageway that would lead them away from the houses when the front door of the end cottage was flung open. A woman dashed down the flagged pathway towards them. A street lamp was bracketed to the corner of the cottage at first floor level. By its light Lee recognised the old lady as Mrs Widdowson, who had a reputation as a witch-like eccentric. He'd never have believed she could move so fast if he hadn't seen her.

'Young man, you're just what I need to deal with a terrible problem in my fruit bushes!' she called to Lee. He was still startled by her appearance and didn't know what to answer; but Joanne instantly had a fit of giggles.

'It's *not* a laughing matter, young lady!' Mrs Widdowson thundered, sternness replacing her agitation. 'You wouldn't be laughing if a stupid donkey was *devouring* your livelihood. It's eating up every one of my lovely fruit bushes. We've got to put a stop to it at once. I need your help.'

'A donkey?' Lee had concluded that she really

15

was as crazy as most of the villagers believed. 'But where's it come from? I mean, are you *sure* it's a donkey in your garden?'

'Oh, don't take my word for it,' she retorted witheringly. 'Come and see it for yourself. But hurry, hurry. I've lost enough bushes already.'

Propping the bike carefully against the gatepost, Lee ran down the path in the wake of the sprightly Mrs Widdowson and Joanne, straight through the long, narrow cottage and into the narrow and even longer back garden. True enough, a donkey was there, chewing contentedly on a bush. As they arrived beside it, the donkey eyed them carefully but not for a second did it stop eating. Its long ears moved back and forth like signalling flags as Mrs Widdowson explained that the beast, as she was now calling it, had already demolished most of the gooseberries and was now attacking the black-currants.

'Pots and pots of lovely jam they were going to make,' she cried. 'Now look at them filling that beast's stomach to bursting!'

Joanne, who'd managed to stop laughing at Mrs Widdowson's phraseology, put her arm round its neck and tried to tug it away from the rows of bushes. Not a centimetre did it budge. Then she tried coaxing it with a carrot she persuaded Mrs Widdowson to sacrifice from her vegetable store: but, plainly, the donkey preferred the taste of fruit

16

to vegetables. Loving entreaties whispered into those wagging ears had no noticeable effect, either. Stolidly, the donkey chewed on through every enticement.

'Look, it must have an owner, it must live near by to have got here, so why don't we find somebody who *knows* it and ask them to fetch it, to take it home?' Lee suggested with what seemed to him to be the brightest thinking of the night.

'Its owner is away and that's why I'm looking after it,' Mrs Widdowson admitted surprisingly. 'It lives in the field beyond the end of the garden. Must have followed me after I'd been feeding it and broken through my fence, the ungrateful beast!'

'Does he have a name?' Joanne wanted to know.

'Clarence. Silly name for a donkey in my opinion but, well, there you are, it *is* a silly donkey and –'

'Look, we can't stay here all night, Mrs Widdowson,' Lee cut in. He was becoming exasperated with their lack of success. Moreover, he was aware that it was getting late and his mother wouldn't be pleased if he wasn't home very soon. 'There's one trick that's bound to work – I was reading about it recently in a book about a lonely trek across the Sahara. If we light a fire under the donkey's belly that'll –'

'You'll do no such thing!' Mrs Widdowson shrieked. 'You'd be arrested for cruelty in no time

– and no doubt the police would say I'd been aiding and abetting. Out of the question.'

All three now stared helplessly at the donkey. Clarence, totally unaware of the dire fate being recommended for him, began to dismantle another bush.

'Oh, but there is another shock treatment we could try,' cried Joanne, suddenly inspired. 'Most animals hate noise, especially a loud, unexpected noise. May I borrow your dustbin lid, Mrs Widdowson?'

With evident lack of enthusiasm for such a notion, the cottage owner nodded. At speed Joanne

went to the bottom of the garden and there found, to her delight, two dustbins. Grabbing the lids, she stole up on Clarence's blind side and then, with melodramatic timing, clashed them together like cymbals.

The effect on the donkey was electrifying. One moment he was munching happily, the next he was galloping frenziedly down the path to his own field, braying in apparent terror. Delighted with her instantaneous success, Joanne followed, still banging away with the lids, to make sure he didn't halt before he was well clear of the garden.

'I think that's quite enough of that,' Mrs Widdowson called out to her. 'The wretched donkey's been removed so you can calm down, young lady. And go and put those lids back on the dustbins. I don't want my sleep disturbed tonight by cats raiding the bins.'

Lee raised his eyebrows and then shrugged his shoulders: Mrs Widdowson hadn't even had the decency to say thank you for the good work Joanne had accomplished. All she could do was find something else to complain about.

'Come on, Jo, let's get off home,' he said, softly but urgently. 'It's late enough already.'

Rather grudgingly, it seemed to Lee, Mrs Widdowson allowed them to pass through her cottage again to reach the alleyway. With exaggerated politeness, they both wished her good night and no further trouble with Clarence. The front door slammed shut behind them and they distinctly heard the noise of a bolt being shot home.

A stride from the gate Lee came to an abrupt halt: so abrupt that Joanne cannoned into him. For a moment or two all he could do was stare with disbelief. He couldn't speak.

His motorcycle had vanished.

Two

'But it can't just have disappeared on its own like that,' Lee said for the umpteenth time in sixty seconds. He still found it impossible to believe the evidence of his eyes.

'Come on, Lee, start thinking intelligently,' Joanne told him as she widened the search area by peering into neighbouring gardens and under hedges. 'Somebody, some *person*, has moved the bike – maybe just for a joke or something. But – '

'Some joke!' Lee exploded. 'That bike's the most precious thing in my life. Anybody who touched it without my permission would be a *criminal*. There's nothing in the world *funny* about having a bike pinched – and it must have been pinched, Jo. Some rotten swine has ridden off on it!'

Joanne frowned. 'I think we'd have heard if somebody started the engine and rode away. I mean, it is fairly loud and – '

'In the din you were making with those lids we

21

couldn't possibly have heard anything else,' Lee pointed out sharply. 'Anyway, they could have just wheeled it down the road for a bit and then started it up there.'

There was nothing to be gained by arguing, Joanne realised. She really had supposed that the culprit was simply having a bit of fun at their expense. Now she was inclined to agree with Lee that the bike had been stolen. Unhappily, when they'd discovered the loss there had been no one in sight who might have been able to explain what had happened. Moreover, the entire place still seemed to be deserted.

'Look, I think we'd better go and report this to the police without further delay,' Joanne suggested. 'They might be able to put out a radio call or something to their patrol cars to be on the look out for the bike. They might even *know* somebody who makes a habit of stealing motorcycles and go and catch him before he can flog it or change its appearance or something. Speed off the mark is always said to be absolutely vital in solving a crime. O.K.?'

'I suppose so,' he responded glumly. 'But maybe we should use Mrs Widdowson's phone and dial 999. That'd be quicker.'

'Oh no! In the first place, the 999 system is for real emergencies, matters of life-and-death. We'd be in worse trouble if we tried that. And in the second place, I very much doubt if the old Widdowson would answer the door to us. Now she's got what she wants she won't want to know us, I'll bet. So, come on, let's get down to the police station.'

The light was on over the front door but it was some time before anyone answered their ring. 'I hope this is a proper inquiry because I was just about to go off duty and I don't like to be disturbed for nothing,' said the man Lee recognised as Sergeant Wilde. 'And, anyway, shouldn't youngsters of your age be safely tucked up in bed by this time?'

'We're not as young as that, Sergeant!' Joanne protested. 'We are both at secondary school. Anyway, we've come to report the theft of a valuable motorcycle. It's just happened so the thief can't be far away yet. If you hurry you – '

'Hang on, hang on! Whose motorcycle are we talking about, to start with? The one who's suffered the loss is the one who should be reporting it.'

'It's mine, actually,' Lee admitted rather tentatively. 'But it's a scrambles bike, you know, for motocross. I'm a member of the Skalbrooke Schoolboy Motorcycle Club. I was just wheeling it home, pushing it past Mrs Widdowson's cottage when – '

'You're sure, lad, you weren't *riding* it home?' the policeman cut in. 'That would be an offence at your age and – '

'Sergeant, if my cousin here had been riding it

23

nobody could have stolen it, could they?' pointed out Joanne, doing some cutting in of her own. 'We both know what the rules are and we abide by them.'

Sergeant Wilde frowned and gave her an appraising stare. He must have approved of what he saw because he didn't pursue the matter of illegal riding. Instead, he asked Lee to describe in detail what had happened and then give a description of the bike. Much of it he wrote down, including the code number that Uncle Ken had marked both under the saddle and under the petrol tank. Momentarily, Lee had been doubtful about disclosing that number but he supposed it would be safe enough with the police.

'Well, I don't rate your chances very high of getting it back,' the sergeant announced eventually. 'You'll be very lucky if you do, young man.'

Lee was staggered by that remark. 'But, surely, it can't be far away – and every policeman will recognise it from that description I've given you.'

This time Sergeant Wilde not only raised his eyebrows; he almost managed a smile. It would, however, have been a wry smile.

'Do you have any idea,' he asked, 'how many motorcycles are stolen in this country every year?'

'Er, no.'

'Well, then, be prepared for a surprise. Because the total is over fifty thousand. And that represents a figure of one motorcycle stolen just about every nine minutes, day or night. But, of course, most of them are taken at night, as yours appears to have been.'

This time, Lee was so astonished that he couldn't make any reply at all. He couldn't understand how the police officer could be so calm about things when motorcycles were being stolen on that scale.

'But most of them will be found, won't they?' Joanne asked hopefully, trying to find some way of comforting Lee.

Very slowly, very solemnly, Sergeant Wilde shook his head. 'Fewer than two thousand, I'm afraid. On average, only one bike recovered for every twenty-five nicked.'

'Yes, but that'll be in big cities, won't it?' Lee said. 'I mean, in a small place like this, well, somebody's bound to spot it sooner or later, aren't they?'

'I hope so for your sake, son. But, you see, most of the thieves act pretty smartly to conceal the evidence. Either the bike's given a new overcoat of paint to disguise it or it's dismantled – cannibalised, in many cases, to provide spare parts for other bikes, making them as good as new. Oh yes, that's quite a racket. So don't put your hopes up too high. Like I said, the odds are stacked agin yer.'

'But you'll do your best, won't you?' Joanne asked anxiously.

'Oh, we *always* do that, young miss, whatever some folk think,' said Sergeant Wilde, smiling at last. 'Yes, of course we'll do all we can to get that green-and-silver monster back on the road – er, the scramble circuit.'

'Thanks very much,' said Lee gloomily. At that moment, he thought he might have seen the last of his beloved bike. It was terrible to imagine some villain taking it to pieces and disposing of the best bits for the highest prices.

'Oh, by the way, we'll let you know if there's any news,' Sergeant Wilde called as Joanne was about to close the front door behind them. 'There's no need for you to call here every day to ask what's happening.'

'In other words, don't come bothering us about a mere scrambles bike when we've more important crimes to investigate,' Lee muttered sarcastically.

In spite of Joanne's reminders that his mother would be increasingly concerned about the lateness of their return, Lee couldn't be hurried on the rest of the way home. He paused constantly, simply to listen, almost praying that he'd hear a recognisable engine note; though he realised that even if he did he was hardly in a position to chase after the bike and catch it up. He tried to believe there was still a chance that *somebody* had hidden it for a joke and that, somewhere along the route, he'd find it again.

Although Mrs Parnaby certainly mentioned the time in a disapproving way she didn't go on about it unduly. She had some news of her own: there'd been a phone call from her husband on the other side of the world.

'All being well, he'll be home next month,' she told them happily. 'He's picking up a new ship, a refrigerator ship, in New Zealand. It was a lovely clear line for once, almost sounded as if he was next door. And he was hoping to have a word with you, Lee. He spent ages talking to Darren instead.'

Lee was wise enough now to keep his thoughts

on that subject to himself. Even if he had been at home when the call came, his father would still have talked longer to Darren.

Dutifully he asked a few questions about his father's recent exploits at sea and then, without giving too much emphasis to the matter, explained that they'd been to the police station to report the probable theft of Lee's bike. Mrs Parnaby was sympathetic but of the opinion that it would turn up soon enough. She wasn't wildly enthusiastic about her sons' devotion to scrambling but she tolerated it; with her husband being away from home so much she was grateful to Joanne's father for all that he did to enable the boys to enjoy the hobby, as she thought of it.

When, at last, Lee went up to the bedroom he shared with his brother, Darren was scanning a horror comic. But he quickly put it down in order to recount the details of the chat he'd had with his father; inevitably, he chortled over the fact that Lee had missed the phone call altogether. Eventually, after he'd exhausted that topic, Darren, the elder by one year and one day, asked whether anything interesting had happened that evening at the Skalbrooke circuit.

Lee, who'd just climbed into bed and switched off his own light, decided he might as well disclose the news of the tragedy now. Darren would have to know sooner or later. So he provided a very brief, edited version of the events since Mr Shearsmith had dropped him off in the village.

He could guess Daz's reaction: and Daz didn't let him down. He jerked upright, eyes wide, expressing first amazement, then scorn. It hadn't taken him long to work out that Lee's loss could be his own gain; with his brother out of the way, Darren would stand a better chance of winning a motocross.

'Well,' he concluded, sounding almost triumphant, 'you're good at losing races, Lee – and now you're just as good at losing a bike!'

'I've won more races than you! And that's what counts,' Lee retaliated. Then he turned over heavily to indicate that the conversation was at an end.

Darren, however, always tried to have the last word. With a fiendish grin he called: 'Well, you won't be winning any more if you haven't got a bike, will you? And who's going to buy you a replacement?'

Lee pulled the sheet up over his head. In the depth of his despair at that moment he could even believe that Darren himself had organised the theft of the beautiful green-and-silver motorcycle.

Three

As the car park began to fill up at the next meeting of the Skalbrooke Schoolboy Motorcycle Club Lee muttered some excuse to the friends who'd brought him and wandered off on his own. He wanted to see as many bikes as possible rolled out of the vans and removed from the trailers. It was, he knew, absurd to think that any of his fellow members of the club could have stolen his machine and then brought it to the track for their own use. Yet he couldn't stop himself from glancing at every transporter bus and trailer just in case a miracle had happened. Naturally, he did it as discreetly as possible. It would be terrible if anyone realised what was in his mind.

For Lee, it had been the longest week of his life: the longest and the darkest. He'd resisted every impulse to visit the police station in the village and inquire how the search was going. Of course, he knew how it was going: because the police hadn't contacted him. So, plainly, the bike had vanished without trace. Perhaps, by now, it was in a hundred pieces, scattered the length of the country, with the vital components contributing to other people's scrambles. But he didn't really believe that. He had to believe that the bike, his bike, was still as he'd last seen it, albeit in someone else's possession.

Now, he headed for the paddock and wondered whether Joanne would turn up. Her parents had returned from their Paris trip the previous day and Uncle Ken had promised to bring Darren to the meeting as usual. No doubt he would have something to say to Lee about the loss of the machine he'd bought for him.

It was the sort of dry, sunny day that, following a week without rain, provided the fast track conditions that Lee liked best. It seemed to him now that even the weather was conspiring against him; had it been pouring down and turning the circuit into a glue-pot he might, just might, have felt a little better. A small crowd was gathering by the control van close to the starting area. Many of the riders, he knew, would be reserves, hoping, probably actually *praying*, for someone not to turn up so that they could compete in the absentee's place. Well, one of them at least was going to be lucky: he or she would be able to ride in the Intermediates' events instead of the brilliant, lightning-fast, stop-at-nothing, internationally famous rider Lee Parnaby. After thinking that up, Lee tried a sarcastic laugh;

31

but it was such a dreadful effort that he nearly choked himself.

Automatically, he paused beside the 'For Sale' tables on which was laid out a great quantity of merchandise of all kinds: sets of riders' leathers, helmets with new-style visors, boots, knee-pads, both new and second-hand, sets of tools for budding mechanics. It was from such a stall, he remembered, that Joanne had bought him a lucky mascot just before he won his first race at the club. He fingered it now in his pocket: a key-ring with a leather tab cut in the shape of a cat. Lee twisted the strip of leather fiercely and decided it hadn't brought him much luck lately. Perhaps he should get rid of it, throw it away when no one was looking; he didn't suppose Jo would actually ask him if he'd still got the key-ring.

'Fancy a new helmet, then, Lee?' a voice inquired cheerfully as he was turning away from the tables. 'The new material this one's made of is terrific. So light you'd hardly know you're wearing it. Go on, give it a try – once you've tried this kind you'll never want any other sort!'

'If I'm not riding a bike I don't need a helmet, do I?' retorted Lee, turning away sharply. 'And I can't ride a bike if I haven't *got* one.'

The tone was savage enough to cause the salesman to blink. In the past he'd sold Lee a number of items of equipment and come to regard him as a pleasant, easy-going boy with a sense of humour. Plainly, Lee Parnaby wasn't his usual self today.

On a low-loader parked at the edge of the selling area stood a 100 c.c. Honda, its red paintwork glistening in the sunlight. Lee couldn't avoid gazing at it wistfully. It was exactly the sort of machine that could carry him to success again in the Intermediates' race. It, too, was for sale – it was actually a second-hand bike – and the thought flitted through his mind that perhaps the owner would consider a hire-purchase deal. He tried to calculate how much would be needed for each instalment. Was there a chance that Uncle Ken would agree to meet the cost?

A moment later Lee shook his head to clear it of such stupid ideas. Darren might have received a favourable response if he'd needed financial help because he was Uncle Ken's favourite nephew – always had been and, presumably, always would be. Originally, Uncle Ken had thought that Darren was the superior rider if only because he was the elder; then, when Lee had proved otherwise by his victories on the track, Uncle Ken had stuck to his first choice because Daz needed support and encouragement as the underdog! That, anyway, was how Joanne had summed up the situation – and she knew her own father pretty well. No, Lee concluded, there was little point in asking his uncle to help him to acquire a new motorcycle. His only

33

hope of riding again was to find the one that had been stolen.

He tried to chat with a few of his pals and rivals but they were really too busy to talk to him: tinkering with the engines of their own bikes or assisting their mechanics (invariably father or brother) to change a tyre or adjust the tension on a chain. Brake and clutch cables were being examined, nuts tightened, plugs given final attention; there was no time for idle gossip. Lee collected a few handfuls of sympathy from those who'd heard of his loss; but he didn't want them. All he wanted was some action. So he slouched away from the paddock, and all the frantic activity of those who were actually going *to race*, and made his way across the track to a vantage point where he could watch the Juniors hurtling towards their own ambitions.

Suddenly, there was a serious spill on the sharp left-handed bend right in front of him. A boy Lee recognised as Andy Appleton had been riding headlong into the corner in his usual fashion; then, at the last split-second, he had a change of heart, tried to brake as he turned the front wheel – and the outcome was inevitable. As Andy went sprawling across the track another bike, hotly pursuing him, cannoned into Andy's slithering machine. The man standing next to Lee leapt over the marker tape and on to the track to sort things out. The woman who'd been standing beside him, holding the flags in her role as a marshal, seemed about to follow when he told her to stay where she was. Lee, however, thought some help was needed to sort out the tangle and prevent a worse pile-up for already there was hardly any room on the track for the following riders to squeeze through and continue in the race.

'Come on, son, come on, you're all right,' the man was assuring Andy as he lifted him bodily from the track. 'You've only got a shaking – be right as rain in no time.'

It was Lee who hauled young Appleton's bike from the centre of the track and then wheeled it to safety. In Lee's opinion Andy had been far too rash in his approach to the bend; on the other hand, the boy who liked to be known as 'Double-A' never lacked spirit and was always willing to have a go at any obstacle. Just as Lee cleared the track two of the slower riders collided right in front of him and so again he went to sort out the problem. Quite by chance, he'd chosen to spectate at the most incident-packed place on the entire circuit.

The St John Ambulanceman who'd been attending to some of the fallen riders was furious with the woman marshal. It was her husband who'd gone on to the track to rescue Andy and, according to the St John man, she'd been so interested in what was going on that she'd forgotten to put up the yellow flag to warn everyone that there was an accident. As a result of her negligence there'd very nearly been a worse pile-up.

'Oh, but I *did* wave my flag! Everybody must have seen it,' the woman protested, looking round for someone who might confirm her story. Her glance fell on Lee. 'You saw what action I took, didn't you? Lee Parnaby, isn't it?'

'Er, I didn't see anything,' Lee, taken by surprise, told her. He didn't want to get involved in a row. 'I was too busy. Sorry.'

He backed away in case she persisted – and bumped hard into somebody.

'Hey, look where you're going, son!' a man called in alarm. 'One accident's quite enough already.'

'Sorry,' Lee muttered again. Then, when he turned round, he saw what the man meant.

Carrying his son, Danny, over his shoulder in fireman's lift style, was Barry Millard, one of the Skalbrooke club's most enthusiastic supporters (he was also rumoured to be one of its wealthiest because he had his own business as a builder as well as a fleet of lorries). Danny was of Lee's age and a long-time rival. At a previous meeting, however, he'd smashed up his ankle, which was in plaster. He wasn't going to miss any of the action if he could help it, however, and that was why Mr Millard was prepared to carry him from vantage point to vantage point.

'How's it going then, Danny?' Lee inquired, glad to escape the attentions of the woman marshal.

'Oh, getting better, I expect. Just wish they'd let me ride, that's all – I mean, Dad could set it in concrete and the ankle'd be fine!'

It was plainly a joke he'd made several times already but Lee dutifully laughed. He couldn't help sympathise with a scrambler who'd broken an ankle. It was almost as bad as having a bike stolen. Still, a cracked ankle would mend eventually but there was no guarantee the missing machine would ever be seen again.

'Thought you'd be in the pits, tuning up your bike for the Intermediates' race,' observed Danny. 'Nothing wrong with you, is there, Lee?'

While Mr Millard settled his son on a convenient mound of grass so that he could watch the racing in relative comfort, Lee sorrowfully related the story of his own tragedy. Mr Millard asked a few pertinent questions about the efforts of Lee and the police and everyone else to trace the stolen bike. Danny said nothing, though his attention didn't seem to wander while Lee was talking.

'Couldn't your Uncle Ken have found a substitute bike for you, Lee?' asked Mr Millard sympathetically. 'I've always thought he looks after you and your brother very well – goes to a lot of trouble to keep you racing.'

'Er, afraid not, Mr Millard.' Lee didn't want to

say anything that could be regarded as criticism of his uncle. 'Uncle Ken and Aunt Sue have been away in Paris for a few days and only just got back.'

'Got your gear with you? Your boots and stuff?' Danny inquired unexpectedly.

'Well, some of it – the essential bits. I mean, I was just keeping my fingers crossed that the bike might turn up and then – '

'If you like, you could ride my spare bike, the Kawasaki. Better for it to be on the move than standing around doing nothing,' Danny offered. He said it in such a casual tone that Lee could scarcely believe he meant it.

'*Honestly*, Danny? You'd let me have it, just like that?'

'Oh sure. You're a good rider so you won't bash it around. Like I said, it might as well be tuned up by racing than sitting in the van. It'll be O.K. if Lee takes it, won't it, Dad?'

Mr Millard nodded emphatically. 'Was just going to suggest the same thing myself. No point in your being immobilised, Lee, when we can help out. In any case, we brought the bike with us for, er, well, for an emergency, let's say. Look, now that you're settled and comfortable, Dan, I'll take Lee over to the car park so he can get the old Green Meany started. Won't be long.'

Before Lee could exhaust himself in uttering endless thanks for Danny's kindness, Barry Millard

39

steered him across the track and in the direction of the paddock and park.

'It's not in bad shape even if I say so myself,' grinned Mr Millard as he lifted the green-and-white Japanese machine out of the van. 'I reckon you could do a lot worse than ride this one, Lee. Anyway, it'll give us all a chance to see what it's capable of.'

Lee reached for it with the reverence he felt for the most powerful and desirable motorcycle in the world. Only a quarter-of-an-hour earlier he'd been thinking of himself as the unluckiest member of the Skalbrooke Schoolboy Motorcycle Club. Now, as a result of literally bumping into Danny Millard and his dad, he was surely the luckiest. Against all the odds, he was going to race again immediately.

'Look, you'd better get over to the control van and let the officials know about the change of bike and so on,' Mr Millard advised. 'Then, pick up your gear. If there's anything extra you need I expect you'll find it in the back of our van. We always keep a pile of spares. Danny-boy can be a bit tough on knee-pads and shoulder protectors! Right, Lee, off you go then. Oh, and just remember – we'll be cheering you on every time you come past us. You'll be giving Danny an extra, personal interest in the racing while he's laid up.'

Lee bounded away with all the exuberance of a spring lamb. He wished that Joanne would turn up so that he could share his joy with her. In fact, it was her father that he met, face to face, as he came away from the control van.

'Ah, Lee, I was looking for you,' Uncle Ken began, his face already creasing into a frown. 'We need to have a serious talk.'

'Sorry, Uncle, but do you think it can wait until after the first race?' Lee answered blithely. 'I need to get the bike warmed up, you see, and well, there isn't much time.'

'Oh, so you've *found* your bike then?' Mr Wragby said in a warmer voice. His face now brightened again. 'Well, that is – '

'Er, no, not exactly, Uncle,' Lee cut in warningly. 'But I'll explain everything later. Oh by the way, did you have a good time in Paris?'

'That all depends,' was the heavy reply. 'It depends on what happened here in my absence. Darren's been telling me all about your – '

'Yes, well he would, wouldn't he? But I'll tell you the *truth* when I've beaten Daz again in this next race.'

Four

Lee was feeling rather less confident about the outcome of the race as he sat astride the Kawasaki, waiting for the elastic tape to zip sideways to signal the start. He had a poor draw in the middle of the line of riders. Because the first bend was an acute left-hander he needed a flying start to pull ahead of those bikes on his left. But, of course, he couldn't be sure just how his new machine would respond when he let it go. On a tight course such as this one the early leaders had a considerable advantage so long as they remained calm. Often Lee had heard it argued that a race on this circuit was usually decided on the first lap. So the first essential was to make a lightning dash from the gate.

Graham Relton, whose supremacy in his age-group Lee had challenged in recent events, was immediately on his left. Behind his visor his eyebrows had visibly shot up on catching sight of the machine Lee was riding. There'd been no opportunity for an exchange of comments but Lee had no doubt at all that Graham would take comfort from the fact that his rival was mounted on an unfamiliar bike. Lee, for his part, had hoped to conceal the change until the race was well under way; then, if he could outwit Graham at some stage, it would be doubly satisfying, not least because Gray perhaps wouldn't recognise the new combination of rider and bike from the rear! Now, of course, that ambition was dashed.

The tension that was always present at these times was tightening its grip on him – and probably every other rider alongside him. He moistened his lips, tried to ease his fingers inside the gauntlets, adjusted the throttle yet again for the perfect take-off and prayed he'd be in luck.

Despite his almost desperate determination to lead the field into the first bend, Lee was actually one of the last to move. Somehow he hadn't seen the tape snap away and it was Graham's surging back wheel that alerted him to the fact that the race had started. Kerry Todd, the throttle-happy girl on his right, shot away ahead of everyone on her Yamaha.

Lee, feeling the rear-wheel spin but achieving no acceleration, bounced on the saddle – and this time the power was there. His heart, though, was sinking as he headed into the cascade of dust sent up by flying tyres. He had made a complete hash of things in his first race on the Green Meany.

Then, as visibility improved and he began to think about his racing line for that first bend, he realised that the bikes ahead of him were slowing and, in one or two cases, turning broadside on to him. In almost the same instant he spotted the red flag being waved vigorously to recall the field. Lee breathed again! There had been a false start. Someone had anticipated the starter's signal and that was why Lee hadn't seen the movement of the tape; and he wasn't alone in that.

Once again the nervous excitement built up swiftly as, with the line re-formed, the riders awaited their dash towards glory – or grief. Lee was worried that his bike wasn't going to provide him with anything like the performance he could expect from his own machine. He suspected there was plenty of power to be called on – Danny Millard wouldn't have tolerated anything less – but it might take time to find out how best to control it. And time was really not on his side.

This time he was alert enough to discern the slight movement of the starter's shoulder as he released the tape. There was no free spin of the back wheel – he was away and helping to create the great cloud of blue smoke from roaring exhausts that would hang above the starting gate for quite some time.

Into the first corner he went as one of the leading batch – hardly a wheel's width behind Graham

Relton. Kerry Todd, too, had got a flier. The Yamaha cut in on Lee as they shuddered powerfully through the angle and quickly built up speed again. Kerry was one of the newer riders in the club and Lee had a lot of respect for her tenacity and courage; she could, however, be dangerously headstrong at some bends where caution really was vital.

The Kawasaki came on strong as Lee risked going for a gap between the two riders directly ahead of him. If he didn't take his chance now it would probably vanish within seconds. He had learned not to hesitate when a genuine opening presented itself. Once again, the Green Meany responded with flowing acceleration and Lee had a trouble-free passage into sixth place.

The boy just in front of him was Robert Beaman, known to every other member of the club as Concorde, or Conky for short, simply because he spent so much time high in the air. Robert really loved a ribbed route because then he could fly all the time; it hardly appeared to concern him that, by spending so much time in the air, he was ruining his chances of success. He enjoyed going upwards and that was that. Lee knew that he could overtake Conky almost at will. So that was one rider ahead of him he didn't have to worry about.

The next real test was the hairpin where Danny Millard and his father were keeping watch.

Although he guessed that they'd give him a wave and a cheer Lee was going to take no risks by responding in any way at all. He'd treat the U-turn with caution and so demonstrate that he was handling Danny's bike with care. The time to throw it about would come when he was in contention for the lead on the final lap.

Although his rear wheel took a knock from a bike that was striving to overtake, Lee negotiated the turn without difficulty and moved up through the gears. He was finding the clutch a little strange but, he supposed, that was to be expected on a new machine. All the same, it seemed to him to be slipping at times. Probably it simply hadn't occurred to Mr Millard to warn him of the Green Meany's individual peculiarities.

The thrusting rider behind him was again making a determined effort to get past and, this time, Lee took a quick glance in an effort to identify him. Much to his surprise, it was Darren. Whether Darren recognised him he couldn't tell. Certainly he gave no sign that he knew who was directly in front of him – or, as Daz himself would undoubtedly put it, obstructing him. What surprised Lee was that his brother wasn't already in the leading group for he invariably got off to a flying start; it was later in a race that his troubles tended to occur. Perhaps on this occasion he'd been caught out by the false start and been unable to achieve a second successive fast break. Now, of course, he would be determined to make up for missed opportunities to keep pace with Gray Relton.

Although he was just as keen as anyone else to win the motocross Lee couldn't resist the thought of keeping Daz at bay for as long as possible. It was a perfectly legitimate tactic to prevent a rival from overtaking you and Lee could just imagine Daz's fury if someone succeeded in holding him off for an entire circuit; it would be all the more pleasurable if Daz didn't know for sure who was responsible – until later, anyway.

Lee was certain he knew just where his brother would attempt to overtake. It would be on an uphill section out of a sharp right-hand corner across the camber. The climb was over exposed tree roots and led to a wooded section where the track naturally narrowed. A burst of power up that stretch should carry any front-runner clear of slower, or down-hearted, opponents. Lee intended to cut Daz off and then have the great joy of soaring away up the gradient – after letting his brother see just who had cut him off! Now that he was racing again, even though it wasn't on his own bike, he was experiencing a tremendous sense of sheer happiness. Apart from one or two minor qualms, he had no doubt now that the Kawasaki was a fine machine, well tuned and capable of putting any rider in the forefront of the field.

With controlled bursts of speed and fractional changes of his racing line, Lee kept just ahead of his brother's Yamaha. He could visualise every grimace and snarl in Daz's repertoire. Well, none of his ferocity was going to help him now because Lee wasn't going to yield so much as a centimetre to let him through.

By now, the leaders were out of sight. Lee supposed that among them would be Greg Shearsmith as well as Graham Relton, Kerry Todd and Concorde Beaman. Soon Conky would be in his element because at the approach to the right-hander there was a series of ripples on a slight downhill run. He would really fly those! With a bit of luck, Lee would follow suit.

Now the track swung away almost lazily to the left and back again and then Lee had the vicious right-hander in his sights. With Daz pushing strongly for an opening Lee opened up the throttle again to give himself the advantage of a slightly longer lead.

He was, he realised, going rather faster than he should to meet such a hazard; but, by this stage, he was quite confident he could cope with the situation. He felt he and the Kawasaki blended extremely well.

Instinctively he braked as the ground suddenly fell away from him. But, as he did so, his thumb rolled away and caught the throttle. With the front

wheel locking and the back thrusting ahead the outcome was inevitable.

Slewing violently, the Green Meany pitched Lee sideways. Astonishingly, he still managed to hold on to the machine and was in the act of pushing himself upright again when Darren cleverly swerved past him. In that same instant, Daz saw who it was – and without further thought put the boot in by kicking his brother out of the way. Later he would claim that he was simply steadying himself as he came close to toppling from his Yamaha because of the tricky manoeuvre he'd had to make.

But even as he crashed to the ground, Lee knew exactly what had happened. He couldn't really blame Daz for what he'd done. After all, he was the one who'd caused Daz's frustration and resultant anger.

Other riders, too, swept by as Lee got to his feet. To his great relief he found that he wasn't hurt in any way, apart from a slight ache in his shoulder. No doubt he'd wrenched a muscle as he tried to keep the bike upright. The engine was still running sweetly, the framework appeared to be unmarked, the rear wheel continued to spin.

'How are you, son?' asked an anxious voice as hands helped him to his feet. 'You were really going a bit crazy there, weren't you? Much too fast for safety.'

'It was a mistake,' Lee tried to explain hastily.

'It's not my bike and I must have touched the throttle when I was actually braking – easy to do if your hand slips. Look, I'm O.K., really. I want to get back into the race.'

No one, at that point, was trying to stop him. Once a rider was seen to be still in good shape and determined to keep riding he was encouraged by the marshals to do so. Luckily, the spill hadn't brought disaster to anyone else and so Lee had plenty of help from onlookers and the St John Ambulanceman as well to get back into the saddle and rejoin the pursuit of the pack. But now, of course, he was one of the tail-enders. His hope of finishing the scramble among the leaders – and ahead of Daz – was now of the slenderest kind.

The shoulder he'd half-landed on, and which he'd once injured before, protested slightly as he lifted the bike through the last of the ripples and then began to build up pace for the attack on the uphill section. This was one of the toughest parts of the track and the juddering effect of riding over the tree roots put a great strain on rider and mach-ine. Lee had known several rivals come to grief at this point and even now a dazed looking boy in a blue helmet who'd parted company with his Suzuki was being attended to by the bushes.

To Lee's dismay, the bike's response when they started on the steep climb was weak. Moments be-fore he'd been sure he had plenty of power and

51

there was no suggestion that the engine was misfiring. Yet the bike seemed to have no zip at all. Even one of the complete duffers went past him with a triumphant air. Lee switched his line to avoid the keenest incline and that helped; so he began to weave instead of keeping an arrow-straight course. All the same, he knew he would never get back into the thick of the action if he had to keep making adjustments like that.

Moments earlier he'd been feeling thankful that Danny Millard and his father hadn't been in a position to witness his disaster at the right-hander; now he rather wished he could ask them whether the Green Meany was usually temperamental on severe uphill sections or was simply being ridden in the wrong manner. Lee was aware that some machines had special peculiarities, just like human beings, and until a rider was used to them he didn't really know what to expect in various situations. Perhaps the Kawasaki needed to be nursed a little before being asked for maximum thrust.

He continued through the wooded area at the top of the hill without further trouble. The track was firm, if rather bumpy in places, and gradually he was able to build up speed and even pass a few stragglers. By now he had no idea at all how the race was progressing but he supposed that Daz would be chasing the leaders hard even if he were not one of them himself. When he recollected

Darren's speed of reaction, and his excellent balance during the skirmish at the bottom of the incline he could only admire his brother's performance. He really hadn't imagined that Daz was capable of producing such skills under pressure.

Shortly he sped past the point where Uncle Ken had stationed himself in order to give Daz any information he could about what was happening during the race – and indicate if necessary when he should close up on those in front. Lee doubted that his uncle realised who was riding the Kawasaki at the moment it went past him. Just as well, Lee reflected; he didn't want to be noticed in a hopeless position.

He had just completed, in very smooth fashion, a fast switchback and was planning to turn on the juice when the race came to an abrupt halt – for Lee Parnaby. It came about quite unexpectedly. Sailing contentedly over the rise of the next fairly shallow incline he was startled to come upon two tangled bikes that were almost completely blocking the track. The riders were on their feet beside the horizontal machines and appeared to be arguing fiercely with one another while a marshal struggled to separate them. The boundary tape had been removed and, it seemed to Lee, the route switched to the right to avoid the squabbling motocrossers.

'Yes, that's the way now, go right, go *right*,' the marshal yelled at him after sensing his bewilderment. He pointed to the gap with his flag and Lee needed no further bidding. After all, like every other member of the club, he was used to obeying the instructions of officials who were conscious of safety requirements above all else.

Almost at once he sensed he'd taken the wrong course: that he'd misunderstood the official's signal. As he bounced over the thick, springy grass that formed a mound in the centre of the circuit he realised that no other bike had travelled that way – or, at least, not as part of the motocross. Too late he remembered from his previous explorations of the area on foot that, on the far side of the mound, were the remains of old quarry workings.

The land fell away at one point like the rim of a cliff.

Desperately, Lee braked hard. The back wheel slithered away from him on the grassy surface and this time Lee was unable to stay with the bike. He was flung sideways and into the tough, thick roots of a gorse bush. The engine cut instantly.

For several moments Lee simply lay where he had landed. Fortunately, his clothing protected him from the spiky gorse. He studied the bike that, he knew now, had let him down. The rear wheel was motionless and, for the first time, Lee really looked hard at the tyre – and saw that the nobbles were practically non-existent. No wonder there hadn't been much grip! That tyre ought to have been replaced long ago.

Oddly enough, both the owner of the bike and the marshal who'd misdirected Lee arrived on the scene at the same moment, but from opposite directions.

'You weren't supposed to come over here, this isn't part of the course,' the official said in an agitated manner to Lee. 'I was trying to channel you round that ridiculous pile-up. Couldn't you see that?'

'But the marker tape was missing,' Lee pointed out. 'I thought there was a good reason why the course had been changed.'

'Yes, that was a mistake,' the man now admitted.

Then, as if to defend his status, he added: 'But a boy of your experience – and intelligence – should have realised that. Everybody else went the proper way. Anyway, you're not hurt, are you?'

Lee shook his head. Satisfied that he'd done all that could be expected of him, the marshal departed sharply to take up his duties again.

'Not your day, is it, Lee, old son?' remarked Mr Millard with a grin. Once again he was supporting his son in a fireman's lift. The restless Danny had decided he wanted to move again to another viewing point. 'The old bike didn't let you down, though, did it?'

Lee wasn't quite sure how to answer. After all, they had been kind enough to lend him the machine in the first place. Mr Millard might be insulted if told that the rear tyre was in a terrible state and should never have been raced on.

'Er, no, it was pretty good really,' answered Lee, trying to sound enthusiastic about the Green Meany. 'Perhaps, though, I didn't quite get the hang of handling it. I mean, I think that's why I finished up here!'

With what he hoped was a convincing laugh he at last got to his feet. Once again his shoulder muscles protested mildly as he lifted the bike and examined it quickly for signs of damage. To his immense relief, it looked fine.

'I'll get it back to the car park for you, shall I?

Now that I'm out of this race there's not much point in going on riding it. I've no chance of picking up enough points to finish among the leaders at the end of the day.'

'O.K., son,' said Barry Millard cheerfully. 'Sorry it didn't work out better for you. But at least you got a bit of a ride.'

Then, for the first time since he'd arrived on the scene, Danny spoke.

'Didn't expect you to get much further than this, anyway, Lee,' he remarked in a matter-of-fact tone. 'Not with a rear tyre as worn out as that one. We knew it wanted changing but we didn't know just how bad it was.'

Lee just stared at him but inwardly he was groaning.

'*Now* you tell me! Well, thanks very much for nothing!' was what he wanted to say. Somehow, though, he managed to keep silent.

Five

The sun was laying an orange carpet across the glistening meadow beside the river as Lee ran along the tow-path. Yet, in spite of that rising sun, there was still a chill in the air and he was already wishing he'd chosen to wear his track-suit instead of T-shirt and very abbreviated shorts. Still, he'd soon arrive at the start of the trim trail on the edge of Sonnington Park and the exercises he'd be doing there would definitely warm him up.

The early morning run was part of his campaign to improve his stamina and strengthen his leg muscles. Even before riding in his first race he guessed, from magazine articles he'd read, that motocross was a tough and demanding sport. Now, from experience he knew it was, and therefore physical fitness was a vital factor in the effort to be a successful rider. Running not only helped to increase lung capacity but strengthened leg muscles – and the legs had to be strong when a rider was directing a powerful bike over energy-sapping scrambles circuits. Lee also underwent a series of exercises with weights on a multigym at a leisure centre but he found that he enjoyed the running part of his fitness programme more than anything. From time to time he paused to do deep breathing routines that also helped what he described to various amused or interested onlookers as 'the oxygen intake situation – you see, how much oxygen you can absorb in a second or so is the real key to success in sport'. He'd yet to come across anyone who tried to deny that.

Of course, the odd self-proclaimed genius such as Darren scoffed at the notion that physical fitness was so important. According to Daz, the top motocross rider needed only skill on the bike and determination to stay at the top. Naturally, he included himself in that category and, at present, he had a point. He had finished runner-up to Graham Relton at the last club meeting when Lee hadn't even finished the course on his borrowed bike. To his own immense and noisy satisfaction, Daz had actually won one of the day's four races, though Gray had been unlucky that time with a broken chain. Inevitably, his brother was still making silly jokes about how 'little Lee has lost his machine and doesn't know where to find it!' It was no longer worth pointing out the stupid repetition within that sentence: if you'd lost something it

59

naturally followed that you didn't know where it was.

As he left the tow-path and ducked under a rail fence bordering the Park he was reflecting that Darren had everything going for him at the moment: as a result of that first victory, he'd been promised a weekend trip with Uncle Ken that included a visit to some Rugby 'sevens' and a sea fishing expedition. Daz's immediate reaction was to announce that he'd return with a record catch. Although Uncle Ken hadn't been too severe about the loss of the bike – apparently it was insured, which was a consolation for him if not for Lee – he'd not extended the invitation to his younger nephew. Lee's time, he'd suggested, might be better spent 'making a proper search for that missing machine of yours'. Lee just nodded obligingly. In any case, he didn't care for team games and he much preferred his fish, complete with chips and vinegar, straight from a shop.

The trim trail was a new venture and although Lee didn't make a great deal of use of it he rather enjoyed watching some of the overweight, flabby adults try to sweat away a few pounds or get some response from almost non-existent muscles. There were three levels of attainment for the various tests, conveniently marked with red, yellow or green spots; but, because he wasn't trying to prove anything, either privately or in public, Lee simply chose those which would aid his own cause – such as the series of logs to be jumped in two-footed fashion, the step-up-and-step-down stile and then, just for fun, the parallel bars set at different heights. That was an exercise that really brought tears to the eyes of some of the joggers, who furtively had a go at one or two of the stiffest obstacles.

Lee exchanged friendly greetings with a couple of young-ish housewives who made a habit of having a morning run just for the pleasure of the outing – both were slim enough not to have to shed excess weight – and then settled down to his routine. Within moments he was glowing with his exertions. Carefully he felt his thigh and calf muscles after each test. He wrinkled his nose. His legs seemed as thin as ever. No extra muscle had developed as far as he could tell. Still, he *felt* quite strong – and the existing muscles didn't ache nowadays even after a long ride – so all must be well. And somebody had once said that *wiry* people were usually the toughest.

With his ankles hooked under a bar on a wooden frame he was carefully counting his way through a set number of sit-ups when a familiar voice interrupted his concentration.

'Hey, that's a terrific sight! Every Skalbrooke scrambler ought to see it. Otherwise, they'd never believe it!'

Lee hastily unhooked himself from the bar and got to his feet. He looked at his cousin in astonishınent; and then, realising how little he was wearing, in some embarrassment.

'Jo! What are you doing here? I mean, how on earth did you know where I was?'

'Oh, how *clever* of you to realise that I could only be here because I was looking for *you*,' Joanne replied with mock admiration. 'I'd clap my hands if I wasn't holding my sides to stop myself shaking to bits with laughter!'

'Come on, Jo,' said Lee, now beginning to get exasperated. 'Something's happened, hasn't it? You're in a – a funny mood. What is it?'

'Lee, I've got some news for you – and I think it may be good news,' she told him in a more restrained manner, though she still smiled. 'That's why I came pedalling down here like mad, to tell you as soon as possible. I knew you came here for a run so I thought I'd check before trying your home. Listen, don't build your hopes too high but it could be that your motorcycle's been found – well, spotted, anyway.'

'What! But where? Who's got it? Can we go and get it back now? Jo, this is terrific and –'

'Lee! I told you – don't get carried away. We could be wrong, very easily. It's got to be checked first, and that's not easy.'

'Oh, come *on* Joanne! There's no need to build up the suspense. This could be the best news I've had for – for years.'

'I'm just trying to be calm and careful, Lee, that's all. It's for your own good. Now just listen without interrupting and I'll tell you what I know. I was talking about you and your bike – just casually, nothing significant, so don't get any odd ideas about my talking about you all the time – now *don't* interrupt, Lee! As I say, I was mentioning it to Carolyn and she said that was interesting because her brother had been talking about a neighbour of theirs who's been riding around the farm on a new bike lately. Carolyn's parents are farmers, the other side of Lingdale, and this neighbour, a boy called Mike Collier, is supposed to be a bit of a wild guy at times. He's quite a bit older than us, seventeen or so, the same as Carolyn's brother, but he looks younger and he's not very big. That's important because the bike's fairly small, according to Carolyn. This Mike is actually using it to round up the sheep and lambs and that sort of thing!'

'What! But that's – well – a crime!'

Joanne grinned. 'It certainly is if it's *your* bike, Lee. Anyway, as I was saying, it's because Mike is using it a lot on the farm that Carolyn's family have seen it quite often. Well, when she told me that I asked her to check on it for me as much as she could – you know, see what colour it is, what make and whether Mad Mike Collier would reveal how he got hold of it. So she did and she rang me last night and the signs are good. Green-and-silver without a

63

doubt, your make and 100 c.c. But Mike himself is saying nothing about how he got hold of the bike, where he bought it or anything of that sort. In other words, he's being deliberately mysterious about its origin. Not much doubt, is there, that he's got something to hide. And that, Cousin Lee, is as much as I know at this moment. But not bad detective work, is it?'

'It's terrific, Joanne, absolutely terrific! I can hardly believe it's true, that's all. I mean, I'd never given up hope that it would be found but I must admit that after all this time without any news of any sort I was beginning to think I was wrong to keep hoping. Just shows, you should never despair. Mum always says that when she hasn't had a phone call from Dad for a long time. By the way, have you told anybody else about this yet?'

'Of course not!' she replied indignantly. 'It's your bike so you should be the first to know. You're the one who's been going through all the agony since it was swiped that night. I'd have phoned you last night but it was late when I got the news and my parents would have been suspicious if I'd telephoned anyone as late as that – Dad might even have casually-on-purpose eavesdropped! So, no, I didn't tell Dad.'

'Good. Knew you'd realise what I meant. Well, that means we can go and get it back on our own without anyone else telling us not to or causing trouble. This guy sneaked it away from us when we weren't looking so we'll do the same thing to him. Seems dead fair, that. Real justice. Now –'

'Hang on a tick! I think you're forgetting something rather vital, Lee.'

He frowned. 'What's that?'

'Well, we don't *know* yet that it's your bike. We can only *assume* that from the evidence and the general, er, circumstances. Before we do anything rash – anything that might be criminal – we've just got to check it out, make absolutely sure it *is* yours.'

Thinking hard, Lee sat down on the sit-ups bench and stretched his legs out in front of him across the path. After a moment's hesitation, Joanne propped her bicycle against a tree on the other side of the path and then squatted down beside him. She hadn't wanted to say so, but she was very pleased that he apparently wanted to include her in his plan to recover the motorcycle.

Methodically, he asked for any other details she might have about Collier and the farm but all she could tell him was that it was called Top-of-the-Moors Farm and located quite close to the Army's practice range, something Carolyn mentioned from time to time. So far as Carolyn knew there was no regular pattern to Mike's riding of the bike; he simply used it when it was helpful in his farm work. She was fairly certain, though, that he didn't ride it away from the farm.

'Well, we've got to go and see it as soon as possible,' Lee announced in a very positive manner. 'So that means this evening, straight after tea. Somehow we'll have to get a close look at it even if this guy Collier isn't using it. You can get away, can't you, Jo?'

'Oh yes – yes, definitely,' she answered at once, trying not to think of the science test that would have to be written up for that evening's homework. 'We can get as near to the farm as possible on our bikes and then, well, make our way on foot. But we don't want to be seen if we can help it. Then no one will guess what we're up to.'

'Good thinking!' Lee said enthusiastically. 'We'll wear some camouflage. Oh, and binoculars could be very useful. Have you got any?'

She nodded. 'Dad has. He takes them on his fishing trips and watches sea birds. Well, that's what he claims. I've got other ideas. Anyway, I should be able to get hold of them for tonight.'

Lee jumped to his feet. 'Great! Right then, let's meet by the church at half-past six. Honestly, I don't know how I'm going to survive the agony of waiting until then!'

'Oh, I imagine the thought of seeing your magical motorbike again will keep you alive somehow,' grinned Joanne as she swung herself into the saddle of her cycle.

Six

The sense of excitement mingling with anxiety that Lee had been trying to suppress all day finally bubbled over as he finished tea. In his haste to leave the table he stumbled against a chair leg, put out a hand to save himself and knocked the butter-dish to the floor. Fortunately it didn't break and the butter picked up only a small amount of fluff from the carpet.

'What on earth's wrong with you today, Lee?' his mother asked as she watched his desperate efforts to remove evidence of the incident from both butter and carpet. 'You've been like a cat on hot bricks all through the meal.'

'Got to go out. Meeting Joanne at half-six, so I don't want to be late.'

'Oh. Oh, well that's good. Going anywhere, er, special?'

'Not really, Mum. Just want some fresh air, so we're going for a bit of a spin on our bikes up towards the moors.'

'Er, well that sounds a good idea, Lee. Give Joanne my love. But don't be back late. Remember you had a very early start this morning. Can't burn the candle at both ends, you know.'

As he had known it would, the reference to the outing with Joanne disarmed his mother. She thoroughly approved of the interest Lee showed in his cousin and the time he spent with her, especially as Darren could hardly be bothered to say a word to her even when she was a visitor in their home. But then, Darren was almost two years older than Joanne. Mrs Parnaby believed Lee's friendship with Jo was some recompense for the generosity her brother-in-law, Ken Wragby, was forever displaying towards her two motorcycle-mad sons.

Lee wasn't surprised that Joanne had arrived at the rendezvous ahead of him; she'd proved several times that she was an excellent time-keeper. She was wearing a heather-coloured sweater and had put her hair up under a bobble hat. From her saddle-bag she triumphantly produced a pair of binoculars.

'Great! But look at this,' Lee told her with equal pride. From under his light pullover he unwound an authentic camouflage jacket in two-tone mud-and-olive. 'Got it from a mate of mine, who borrowed it from his brother who was in the Army for a couple of years. Cost me a fair bit in cash and promises of free rides on the bike when I get it back but I reckon it's worth it. If anybody notices us they'll think I'm a soldier off-duty and you're my girl friend for the night.'

'Gee thanks, I never thought you'd ask!'

'Come on,' he said quickly, worried that she might take the idea seriously. 'Let's get moving. The sooner we get there the more likely we are to see something.'

They pedalled briskly down the main street of the village, and though it crossed both their minds as they passed Mrs Widdowson's cottage that but for her trouble with the donkey they wouldn't have needed to set out on such a journey, neither of them mentioned it.

After a couple of miles they turned off the highway on to a narrow, deeply rutted dirt track that was obviously chiefly used by farm vehicles. Lee remarked jocularly that it would have served as a motocross course – if they'd been looking for one. After that they had to concentrate on conserving their breath for a hard climb out of a crater and Lee wished he could call on the power of his favourite engine instead of his legs. Beyond the rim of the crater they came across the first warning signs about the dangers of encroaching on the Army firing range which was spread over a large area of the moorland. Sometimes it was used for target practice by armoured vehicles, and the public was ordered to stay well clear of the boundary posts whenever red flags were flying to indicate that shooting was taking place.

Eventually the ground began to drop away and form into hollows and shallow-sided valleys. The bleakness of the upper slopes gave way to attractive grazing land and fields, bordered in some cases by dry-stone walls.

'That's where Carolyn lives,' said Joanne, pointing to a neat collection of buildings beside a tumbling stream. 'So the Colliers' place must be just over that brow.'

'Thank God for that,' replied Lee, glad of a pause even if it lasted only a second or two. 'I don't know how I found the energy to get as far as this!'

A couple of minutes later, however, his tiredness vanished as he gazed down on the farm where he believed his beloved motorcycle was hidden; because, distantly, he could hear an engine note he was positive he recognised.

On such a still evening sounds travelled a long way in the clear air and so it was some moments before the motorcycle came into view through a gap in the hedge surrounding one of the lower fields. By now Lee and his cousin were lying flat in a shallow depression. Lee trained the binoculars on the scene below but he hardly needed a second glance to know that the bike was his. Apart from the fact that the number plates bearing his personal number in white on a blue

background had been removed it was just as he'd last seen it.

He wanted to leap to his feet and cheer with his joy at seeing it again; but somehow he managed to restrict his delight to squeezing Joanne's arm and nodding furiously. She, of course, was just as happy as he was but something about the way the bike was being ridden puzzled her.

'Why is he going so slowly?' she whispered. 'Is he carrying something on the tank?'

Lee, who'd been too busy scrutinising the machine itself to take much notice of the rider, studied the scene again.

'It's a lamb!' he exclaimed a second later. 'It's a black one, too. He seems to be, well, almost cuddling it.'

She laughed. 'Well, it would be black, wouldn't it? I mean, anybody who could pinch your bike and just swan around on it like that is obviously the black sheep of his family! Oh yes, and they're called Collier, too, aren't they!'

After that it was difficult for her to suppress her fit of giggles. Although appreciating the joke Lee was far too intent on watching the rider's progress to add any comments of his own.

Much to his surprise, the bike was taken straight into a large barn on the far side of the yard. When, a few moments later, the rider emerged he was still carrying the lamb very carefully. He headed for the

72

low, stone-built farmhouse and this time he didn't re-appear.

Although they kept watch for another quarter-of-an-hour, until the light began to fade as quite heavy clouds rolled up from the west, no one else was seen around the buildings. At one point, however, a typical black-and-white sheepdog limped across the yard as if taking a last sniff around before retiring for the night.

'If that was Mike Collier he acted in a very gentle way with that lamb,' Joanne remarked in a surprised tone. 'Not at all as I expected from Carolyn's description of him as a wild character. Can't be all bad, after all. I expect he's acting as the shepherd. That poor old sheepdog looks as though it's been hurt recently – or maybe it's just getting to the geriatric stage of life.'

Lee wasn't interested in such sentimental reflections. He had more pressing matters on his mind.

'Look, we could just sneak down there as soon as it gets really dark, grab the bike and ride off,' he suggested. 'I mean, if we just tell the police where the bike is *they* will come and collect it. But they'll hold on to it as evidence until the case comes up in court. So I won't be able to ride it for ages. You see, I asked a guy at school, whose father is a lawyer, what happened when the police recovered stolen property. He gave me all the details. That's why

73

we've got to act for ourselves, Jo, and not get the police involved.'

She nodded. 'I know. I made some inquiries as well, Lee, just in case we were lucky enough to find your bike. It might even be difficult to prove that it really *is* your bike, even though *you* know that it is. The engine number may have been removed. But we can't just go and collect it tonight – no, hang on, Lee, let me finish. And remember, we've got to keep our voices down. Sounds carry in the open like this.'

Joanne paused, marshalling her thoughts. 'There are several reasons. One, it will soon be really dark and we can't risk riding it back to Lingdale over the moors in pitch-black conditions. Two, we can't just abandon our push bikes or manage to ride three bikes between us. Three, we know Mike Collier is up and about and probably the rest of his family are, too. They'd react fast if they heard the bike's engine and give chase. Remember, they wouldn't know we were just reclaiming your property. They'd suspect we were burglars! So there'd be a lot of fuss and we might not even get home tonight. And one last thing: I'm not used to getting up early in the morning like you and I must admit I'm now feeling pretty exhausted. I need my sleep tonight, Lee!'

He was on the point of yawning himself but he quickly covered that up by running his fingers

74

through his thick helmet of honey-coloured hair and then scratching his scalp. Moreover, he'd been aware that his plan of action contained a few flaws.

'So what do *you* reckon we should do? And don't forget I want that bike to myself as soon as possible. I need to gets lots of practice in if I'm going to be chosen for the Inter-Club Championship. You know that's my great ambition.'

'Yes, I know all about that, Lee, and I'm taking it into account. Well, my idea is that we should make a dawn raid – no, not tomorrow but maybe the day after. Then we can really take them by surprise. We were learning in history about how armies attacked at first light and took the enemy completely by surprise. I know people on farms get up early but we can beat them to it with good planning. Also, I'm going to ask Carolyn to help by getting us some inside information about the layout of the farm and things like that. She may have been in that barn and know where a bike is kept – oh, and whether the door is locked. So what do you think of that?'

It appealed to him, especially the concept of making an early start. In any case, his brain was getting too tired to try and improve on the plan.

'It's great,' he told her with all the enthusiasm he could muster. 'We'll work out the details tomorrow. So, come on, let's get off home.'

By the time they reached the village they were

almost too weary to say good night to one another. Even so, Lee didn't find it easy afterwards to drop off to sleep. He couldn't stop thinking about the happiness he would experience when reunited with his bike.

It never occurred to him that something might go drastically wrong with their plans.

Seven

'I guessed Carolyn would be looking out for us this morning,' Joanne said with evident satisfaction as, two days later, she and Lee arrived at the farm. 'Look, she's up there at that first floor window, the end one on the right.'

Lee glanced up and could make out a dark-haired girl, apparently wearing a dressing-gown and with her arms tightly folded as if to ward off the cold. After briefly returning their wave she mimed the posture of sleep and then jerked a thumb over her shoulder.

'Must be her sister who shares her room,' Joanne explained. 'Otherwise I expect Carolyn would have been down to make a cup of tea for us. Pity she can't. I mean, dawn raiders are always supposed to go into action on a hot drink, aren't they? Or is it brandy!'

'I don't suppose,' said Lee heavily, 'that you'll be making jokes when we really start the action at Collier's place.'

'I only do it to help keep my courage up,' admitted Jo as lightly as she could manage. 'Anyway, better get the bikes into the tack room over there and then get on our way. It's getting lighter by the minute. I'd never have guessed the sun really got up as early as this.'

It was Carolyn who'd suggested that they leave their cycles at her farm when they carried out the mission that Joanne insisted on describing as the dawn raid. She'd promised that the cycles would be safe until they were able to retrieve them either that evening or at the weekend. That had neatly solved their problem of how to get to Top-of-the-Moors Farm at daybreak, though there'd still been the worry of waking early enough to set off in the dark. Fortunately, they'd both been able to get hold of alarm clocks (in Lee's case he swore he hadn't slept all night, anyway).

By dint of shrewd yet casual questioning of friends and contacts the ever-helpful Carolyn had discovered that Mike Collier was claiming, when asked, that he'd picked up the motorcycle by chance one evening when attending a party given by a group of young farmers at The Dog and Partridge Inn at Lingdale. His tale was that he thought it had been abandoned and as no one had come forward to claim it he now regarded it as his property. Naturally, Lee was furious when he heard that and Jo had some difficulty in calming him down. But it

78

just proved, he said, what a cunning swine Mike Collier was and how he might have outwitted the police if they'd tried to reclaim the machine.

As they now left one farmyard and headed for another Joanne felt her nerves begin to jangle again. Her fingers tightened on the straps of the haversack she was carrying on her back: it contained some basic tools and a plastic bottle of fuel in case the bike ran out at a critical point in the escape. It had been agreed that they'd both ride but, of course, Lee couldn't have the haversack because then it would come between them. She kept glancing at the sky, watching the streaks of light widening as the day woke up.

They were wearing their camouflage gear again and although Joanne had put on a second sweater she still felt chilled; but that, she supposed, might be caused by apprehension. So far everything had gone almost too well; they hadn't met a single snag. Lee's confidence had waned a little in the interval since the first visit to the area of the farm but now it was advancing with the morning. From time to time he almost trembled with the joyous anticipation of riding his motorcycle once more.

Cautiously they came over the brow. There was no sign of life below; so, after an exchange of glances, they began the descent. They kept as close as possible to a meandering stone wall, in the hope that it might help to mask their approach should anyone glance out of one of the farm windows at the front. But, as far as they could tell, all the curtains were still drawn.

When they reached the corner of the yard Lee whispered 'Good luck, then, Jo'; and his cousin went ahead on her own. It had been agreed that she should check first whether the sheepdog, Luke, was in the barn. If so, she had a biscuit to give him as well as a friendly pat and a quiet word. Once again it was Carolyn who'd supplied the details about the dog; apparently it had a mild manner and would react favourably even to a stranger if offered a sweet biscuit. Luke was rather infirm now but had his own warm corner of the barn, which was never locked at night. Such lack of security seemed unwise to a town dweller but Joanne was thankful for it on this occasion.

Softly she called to the dog as she pushed open the door, and then winced as it gave a slight creak. Next moment a warm muzzle was thrusting into her hand for the biscuit.

'Well done, Luke, well done,' she told him, ruffling his coat. 'Yes, you really are an old softie, aren't you? But I'm really glad you are!'

He limped after her, back into the barn. Joanne had brought a torch and she needed it to help locate the motorcycle; it was in a stall at the far end of the building and covered by a horse blanket. She wasted no time examining it; that was Lee's job.

'Still all clear,' he told her as they changed places in the yard. 'I suppose if you're just looking after sheep you don't have to get up so early.'

That had occurred to Joanne but she hadn't wanted to raise false hopes by mentioning it earlier. Lee, taking the torch from her, went into the barn to check the bike and then move it into the open while she remained on watch. It had been decided that Lee shouldn't start the bike up in the barn unless a real emergency arose. If it could be wheeled out of earshot of the farm before they attempted to ride it then so much the better.

'It'd be marvellous, wouldn't it, if Collier went into the barn to get the bike and discovered somebody had *stolen* it in the night!' Lee had exulted when the raid was planned. 'That'd be real biter-bit justice.'

To his great relief, the bike appeared to be in perfect condition. If anything, it was cleaner than when he'd last ridden it. He couldn't hold back a surge of emotion now that he was touching it again. He ran his hand lovingly over saddle and tank and frame. Then, mindful of how vital every minute might be, he eased it out of the stall and wheeled it across the barn. He could tell that the tank was at least half-full of what a lot of the scramblers called 'go-juice' and so it seemed the supply they'd brought wouldn't be needed.

As he reached the doorway he paused to look in all directions, fearful that Jo might not have spotted that someone was keeping watch on the barn. Even though he was merely removing his own property it was difficult not to feel that he was acting like a criminal. All appeared clear, however, and Jo, looking gleeful, came across to close the huge door behind him. Luke watched, wagging his tail.

Lee's fear now was that the dog would start barking the moment they were clear of the farm buildings; or – and that might even be worse – chase after the moving bike as if trying to round it up like a wayward ewe. Jo, however, had anticipated that possibility and was keeping a supply of biscuits with which to quieten Luke at the critical moment.

Walking on either side of the bike they very slowly made their way down a sunken lane that ran beside the stream to the side of the farmhouse. In rather less than a hundred metres they should be out of sight of anyone looking out from any of the buildings. Luke had halted at the point where the lane inclined sharply downwards: he watched, still gently swishing his tail, with an air of some sadness. Jo was still praying that he wouldn't suddenly break into a furious round of barking. She wasn't sure what to expect of sheepdogs.

'Just keep your fingers crossed – everything crossed – that the engine fires first time and we can get a fast start,' Lee said to her in a whisper, as if they still might be overheard.

'Fast from the gate – you're good at that, Lee,' she encouraged him. 'Don't worry, I'm sure we'll make it now as long as we don't take silly chances.'

Walking the bike and keeping upright on such stony, difficult terrain was tiring work. Lee shifted his grip several times and kept looking back to see just how far they'd come. They'd agreed on a certain minimum distance they should travel before starting the engine; that had been an essential part of the plan and Lee knew he shouldn't attempt to change it. All the same, he was still feeling very nervous. He knew he'd feel a hundred times better as soon as he was in the saddle and heading as fast as possible for home. It would be as thrilling as going flat out for victory on the last lap of a moto-cross.

Now the lane flattened out and Lee pulled the bike across to the right and on to the plateau of moorland. Joanne showed him that her fingers were crossed as tightly as she could manage. She glanced behind her but could see nothing of Top-of-the-Moors Farm.

In the stillness of the morning the throaty roar of the engine as it came to life sounded deafening. Instinctively, Joanne swung round through 360 degrees to check whether anyone had been alerted. She expelled a long breath when she saw that they still had the landscape to themselves.

'Come on, come on, Jo!' he told her excitedly as he prepared to rocket away across the moor. 'I think we've made it! Fantastic!'

Even before she could settle on to the rear part of the seat Lee was accelerating through the gears. The old familiar sensations of speed and power and triumph came flooding back and suddenly it seemed to him that he and the bike had never been parted. When they were both at their peak, or just approaching it, they were one. He had always felt that; or, rather, he had felt it since the start of his success as a scrambler.

He was remembering the theory, so often proved to be true, that a motocross was won with a rapid start – and won in the first lap. Well, he'd made a flying getaway from the lonely farmhouse and now he could see no obstacle ahead of them. Whatever use Mike Collier had made of the bike there was no doubt in Lee's mind that the young farmer had kept it in good shape. It felt as good as it had always done; the response when he shifted up a gear was immediate and electric. The ride home was a trip to be enjoyed.

The sudden eruption of earth on the skyline some distance away took Lee by surprise. A split second later he heard the heavy 'crump' of an explosion. Before he could decide what he should do another fountain of earth shot skywards several hundred metres to the right of the previous explosion; and this time the noise was much louder. Automatically, he swerved away to the left and reduced speed.

'What's going on?' he yelled over his shoulder.

Joanne was swallowing hard. Only a few moments earlier she had noticed the red flag fluttering lightly on one of the posts they'd sped past. At the time it hadn't occurred to her what it meant. But now she knew.

They were in the Army firing range; and they'd arrived while a deadly exercise was in progress.

'We've got to get out of here, Lee,' she shouted into his left ear. 'The Army have started a full-scale war or something with live ammunition. And we're on their land!'

He braked immediately, controlling the skidding

85

rear wheel with all his usual aplomb in spite of his astonishment at what he'd heard.

'But – aren't they supposed to let the public know before they start shooting?' he said. 'I mean –'

'They did,' she replied flatly. 'Red flags are flying on the boundary markers. I saw one some way back but I didn't think what it meant. Lee, we've just got to get away from here as fast as possible.'

'We can't go the way we've come,' he pointed out, 'because then we'd probably meet the Colliers searching like mad for the bike!'

As he spoke another explosion sent a column of earth and stones mushrooming into the sky: and this time the 'ker-rump' was a great deal louder.

'We'll go in that direction, away from the bombs,' Lee said decisively. He was thoroughly frightened, too, but he knew he had to control his fear if they were to escape. 'I expect they're mortars. They're not as bad as they look. Listen, I'm going to be riding at full chat, so sit tight. O.K.?'

She nodded as brightly as she could manage – and then braced herself for the surge of power as they started off again. On such springy terrain, the bounce was higher than she'd expected. Much as she'd have liked to put her arms round Lee's middle, she was determined not to: he had enough distractions as it was. The haversack was bumping a little on her shoulders, threatening to unbalance her, and she thought of getting rid of it. However, with the extra distance to be travelled they might after all need the spare fuel. By now the sun was well up and it was going to be a beautiful day. If, that was, they survived it. . . .

The land began to slip away to their left and Lee realised they were on the rim of a giant crater. On the lower slopes the vegetation was thicker and momentarily he thought of descending because surely they would be safer down there.

Then his eye was caught by a sudden movement away to their right. Cantering towards them was a uniformed figure on a horse. His first thought was that the man was coming to their aid: his second, that if they allowed themselves to be stopped and spoken to by any soldier, they'd be in trouble, if only for trespassing on Army land. Lee promptly swerved away to his left, down the slight slope under the rim and headed for a line of sturdy bushes that might screen them from a pursuer. In this kind of landscape he was in his element because it tested his skills as a scrambles rider.

Joanne hadn't noticed the horse and rider and so she supposed that Lee was simply using the crater as a temporary shelter. As they emerged from the bushes they neatly hurdled a narrow stream and then found themselves on a distinct pathway that appeared to meander along the side of the hollow. Lee decided they might as well follow it; with luck it would lead them away from the firing range – and the soldier on horseback. Soon they were climbing, though the gradient was only slight.

'Look, there's a man on a horse on the skyline!' Joanne called excitedly. 'We're safe!'

That wasn't Lee's reaction. In his eyes, the mounted soldier was almost as threatening as the explosions. Obviously, he was intending to cut off their escape. Lee realised he must have really galloped hard to reach that point on the rim of the crater so much ahead of them. But Lee had no intention of being caught. Deftly he changed gear, turned off the track and bumped over a tiny ridge of stones and rough ground. By now, Joanne had no option but to cling to him to prevent herself being bounced off the bike.

As he went through 180 degrees the bike began to slip on loose soil on the steep slope but Lee kept it going with a burst of power; and a final thrust enabled him to regain the pathway. But then, next instant, he was forced to skid to a halt.

For completely blocking the track was another soldier on horseback.

Lee felt utterly defeated. He would never have imagined that there would be *two* horsemen. Between them, they'd outflanked him. And now, right on cue, the other one was coming down the path towards them: a sergeant with a red band round his cap and riding a handsome chestnut. His eyes were as dark as gun barrels and for several moments he simply stared at Lee and Joanne without saying a word.

'Were you trying to get yourselves killed, then?' he asked at last.

Lee tried to moisten his lips. 'We'd no idea when we set off that there was going to be shooting and bombs exploding.'

'And what do you think the red flags mean? Don't tell me you've never read the warning notices plastered up all over the place.'

'We didn't see them, er, until it was too late. But we were trying to get out of the way now. I've lost my way, that's all.'

Joanne wanted to help him out but she couldn't think of anything to say that would be of any use. Perhaps it would be best if she kept quiet – a silent admission of guilt might curb the sergeant's wrath. He had, she recognised, every right to be angry.

'You're joyriding, lad, that's what you're up to!' declared the sergeant savagely. 'And it could have been the last ride of *any sort* you'll ever have.'

'That's not true,' Lee retaliated spiritedly. 'We were recovering my motorcycle from the guy who stole it – that's why we're out here at this time of the morning.'

This time the sergeant chose to ignore what to him was a very obvious lie. He'd already sent a message through his walkie-talkie about the trespassers so that there would be a cease-fire until they'd been apprehended. But he didn't want to delay the resumption of the military exercise any longer than necessary. The kids had been stupid, criminally stupid, in his opinion, and had to be taught a lesson.

'If we hadn't been on patrol this morning and spotted you sneaking across our territory you probably *would* have been killed,' he now told them in a very cold, precise tone. His horse, which had been getting a little restive, suddenly became as stationary as a statue. It, too, had detected a change in the sergeant's mood. 'Now, I want you both off this land at the double – and we're going to follow to see that you do as you're told. But before you go Corporal Jackson here is going to take down your names and addresses and the names of your schools. Then your parents and head teachers will be hearing from my Commanding Officer. And I've no doubt the C.O. will recommend some proper punishment for your misconduct. Some good military discipline is what you two need.

'Right, Corporal, let's have their names in the book, then.'

Lee swallowed hard and gave his name and the other details demanded. It had occurred to him to provide a false name and address but he suspected the Military Police sergeant would have some means of double-checking his identity and thus an additional misdemeanour would simply result in a more severe punishment eventually. When Joanne supplied her own details she added, defiantly, 'We're cousins, in case you're wondering.' But neither of the soldiers made any comment on that disclosure.

As soon as the corporal finished writing the sergeant began to issue instructions. It appeared that, after all, they weren't so very far from the boundary of the firing range and if they followed the track alongside the marker posts they'd come out on to a minor road that would lead them back to Lingdale Village. First, though, they were escorted out of the crater.

'Off you go, then,' said the sergeant after pointing out the marker posts on the skyline, 'and remember we shall be right behind you till you're off our territory. And just make sure you don't come back – ever – whether the red flags are flying or not. Then you won't be in danger of getting blown up.'

Within a few minutes they reached the road – and freedom. Lee had steeled himself not to look back; and, although he wasn't aware of it, of course, Joanne had done exactly the same. Now, though, Lee paused to express his profound relief at their escape.

'Honestly, I thought they were going to throw us straight into an Army prison camp or something! And even those horses looked as if they'd like to bite our heads off. Terrific size, weren't they?'

Joanne nodded eagerly. 'I don't think we have much luck with four-legged animals, you know. I mean, it was that blooming donkey that was the start of all our troubles, wasn't it?'

'You're right, Jo! I've always preferred two wheels to four legs. To start with, they're faster. Well, *these* wheels are. So, come on, let's speed off home. Then I can get down to the serious business of practising for the Inter-Club Championship races.'

Eight

'How is it, then?' Greg Shearsmith inquired, managing to produce a lop-sided grin as he spoke.

'Terrific – just as good as ever. I don't think that guy Collier messed it up at all but your Dad's an absolute miracle worker with the spanner,' Lee replied with unforced enthusiasm. 'I reckon my bike's in better shape than your face, Greg. Are you *really* sure you're fit enough to ride this afternoon?'

'Yeah, I'll be O.K. I've raced when I've had worse injuries than this one and *still* finished in the first three. I'm aiming to get my hands on that winged trophy for the Best Rider in the Championship, so one little knock on the head isn't going to stop me. No way!'

Lee shrugged and turned away to make some apparent adjustment to a cable. He owed a considerable debt to the Shearsmith family and so he didn't want to say too much. It was typical of Greg to be so dismissive about a personal injury but Lee

93

suspected that this one was just as bad as it looked; it had happened while Greg, attempting as usual to take a near-impossible jump in spectacular fashion, had crashed during a private practice session. Of course, a facial injury wouldn't be obvious during the Championships when he was properly helmeted but his fitness to ride in a fierce competition at speed was surely in doubt. That was particularly so at Terncliff, one of the toughest courses any of the Skalbrooke riders had ever seen.

It had been constructed on a wooded hill that resembled, as Graham Relton, Skalbrooke's captain, had put it, 'the side of a Swiss mountain – and the *steepest* side at that!' Because of a continuing lack of rain the terrain was exceptionally dry and, during practice that morning, clouds of red dust had risen skywards.

All the same, it was a track Lee was eager to test his skills on at racing speed: the jumps and tight turns on the downhill stretches were exactly what he'd been practising at the start of the season. Perhaps, he'd been reflecting, his luck had changed at last. He'd been selected as one of Skalbrooke's six top riders for the Intermediates and had he been allowed to choose his own course for the Championship he'd have picked Terncliff. Even Uncle Ken was smiling at him again (though, of course, it was too much to expect that he had ousted Darren as their uncle's favourite). Apparently Uncle Ken had actually enjoyed his visit to Top-of-the-Moors Farm, according to Joanne who'd lost no time in relating the known details to Lee. Mr Wragby had gone to the farm to 'wipe the floor' with Mike Collier and his family, and, seemingly, had done just that most effectively. As predicted, young Collier had protested that he'd just found the bike and was intending to hand it over to the police when he had time. As a result of Uncle Ken's threats, however, it was unlikely Collier would lay his hands on anyone else's machine ever again. 'Dad loves a good scrap, especially when he knows he's going to win by a knock-out,' Jo concluded her report. 'Oh yes, and he was quite impressed with the way you – and I, she says modestly – located the bike and got it back all on our own. I suspect he knows Darren wouldn't have managed such a feat.'

Lee now glanced across the paddock to where his brother was standing with Uncle Ken. Daz had said very little about Lee's success in retrieving his bike and Lee supposed that Daz was a bit worried about the resumption of their rivalry on the racetrack. Even though both were officially riding for Skalbrooke against the best scramblers from other clubs it was inevitable that the brothers would be equally determined to finish ahead of each other, whatever their fate overall. Moreover, Lee hadn't forgiven Daz for his hurtful remarks during the period he thought he'd lost his bike for ever.

Quite a crowd was gathering round a boy called Duncan McGlew, a Scot who had only recently joined the Terncliff Club and brought with him a reputation for high speed and high skills on grass tracks. Duncan, a remarkably thin, wiry boy with a mane of carroty hair, seemed to have collected a sizeable personal fan club already and he'd been pointed out to Lee by another rider the moment he appeared on the scene.

'From the way he's been going in practice, they think it's going to be a case of Duncan-first-and-where-are-the-rest?' related Nathan Pike, a member of the neighbouring Rockleigh Youth Motorcycle Club and also one of the fancied competitors in the Intermediates.

'Well, if you make sure you put him out of the race I'll look after the others, Nat,' Lee replied with a grin. He rather liked the Rockleigh rider who concealed a fierce determination to win under a gentle, often amused, manner. 'Then you and I can finish first and second.'

'Just as long as *I* am first and *you* are second,' Nathan responded. 'Though I won't object if you're only a wheel-length behind at the line – it'll make it look as though you're *nearly* as good as me!'

There was no time to continue that sort of conversation because the Juniors were on the last lap of their race and so the Intermediates were rolling up to the starting line. Just as Lee was about to pull down his goggles Uncle Ken hurried across for a final word.

'All the best, Lee. I'll be shouting for you all the way. So have a great ride.'

Lee nodded his thanks. He was glad his helmet must conceal the surprise he felt. Normally Uncle Ken had time only for words with Daz. Perhaps, Lee reflected, his uncle was trying to make up for the absence of Joanne who hadn't been able to avoid accompanying her mother on a shopping trip to London. He missed Jo more than he would admit; but, after all, she had shared most of his adventures and successes and she seemed to bring him luck.

The blue haze above the line of exhausts thickened as engines were revved again and again. All eyes, of course, were on the taut tape that would spring sideways to signal the start. Darren, in his distinctive black-and-yellow helmet, had lined up next to his brother. He, like every other rider, was praying for a brilliant getaway and a real chance to prove that he was the Tiger of the Track he so often imagined himself to be.

Greg Shearsmith, striving to get a flier, nudged under the tape, got a severe reprimand from the starter and had to be hauled back more than a metre by his father. As always, the ebony Shear-smith Special was in immaculate condition. Harry Shearsmith, though, had given every bit as much attention to Lee Parnaby's green-and-silver machine and Lee knew that if he failed to win the race it wouldn't be for mechanical reasons.

The tension had crept into Lee's shoulders and he could feel the tightness in muscles at the base of the neck. Like every other ambitious rider, he was affected by nerves as the countdown began before a race; but this event, his first Inter-Club Championship, was a very special occasion. He was determined to make it a memorable one.

Because he was close to the starter's left hand he sensed the movement a fraction of a second before the elastic catapulted out of sight.

The race was on!

Lee's initial acceleration was superbly timed. He'd made the fast start he'd prayed for – and yet, amazingly, Duncan McGlew was ahead of him. Somehow the boy a newspaper had inevitably dubbed 'The Flying Scot' had seized the initiative and was already hurtling towards the first downhill turn with Lee as his nearest rival.

For two of the riders there was disaster even before that left-hander was reached. A Yamaha in the hands of a boy who'd become too throttle-happy in his anxiety to get a flier reared almost like a rocket; and a Terncliff rider alongside him, swerving to avoid a wavering Honda, crashed straight into the Yamaha's fork as it came down. Momentarily the starter thought of stopping the race because it seemed that the fallen pair must be badly hurt. Parents and other helpers, however, were already on the track and rapidly sorting out the trouble. Nonetheless, both riders were too shaken to continue.

Unaware, of course, of what was going on behind him, Lee went in pursuit of the green-helmeted McGlew, blasting confidently over the first jump and then bouncing easily over a rib-like series of half-exposed roots. The pace was the hottest most of the spectators had ever witnessed.

Lee was thankful to have made such a great start but he was keen to know how far he was ahead of such obvious rivals as Graham Relton, Nat Pike and Greg Shearsmith. Because the course was downhill and without a sharp turn for almost a hundred metres he had no way of knowing where the rest were. He would have liked to sneak a glance over his shoulder but he knew that could be fatal.

McGlew, welded to sheer speed like every other grass track racer, seemed set to establish a new record for a Terncliff lap. His lead was already substantial and the exhilarated crowd was plainly on the side of the Flying Scot as he zipped round the treacherous first hairpin. He took it so well that some spectators actually applauded, an almost unheard of compliment at that stage of a race. Lee, following in his wheel-tracks and straining to see through the mushrooming dust, had his engine screaming in third as he attempted to slice into Duncan's lead.

Graham Relton, who'd suffered in the congestion at the first turn, was pushing against Nathan Pike for third position. It was unusual for Graham to be anywhere but out in front but for once he'd not made the best of starts. The top Skalbrooke trophy winner, he was always realistic about his riding and he wouldn't blame his bike for his present position. He knew his concentration had lapsed a fraction at the start. But that only made him all the more determined to make up the lost ground as quickly as possible. His supporters would think he was unwell if he wasn't soon in the lead!

Nat was just as positive in his approach and he wasn't going to yield so much as a centimetre to the Skalbrooke champion. So, for the moment, Nat was more concerned with keeping Graham at bay than with overtaking the pair ahead of him. To Nat, motocross was a tactical exercise, not a fairground brawl.

The four leaders had drawn well clear of the rest of the field, who were bunching up dangerously. Greg Shearsmith, for one, was feeling particularly frustrated as he tried to break out of the pack. But the two riders directly in front of him were adopting a cautious policy in the dusty conditions of this fast, switchback course. Alongside him, the self-styled Tiger of the Track was also snarling furiously at not being able to make the progress he knew was necessary at this stage. The sight of his brother so far ahead of him already was tormenting Darren Parnaby.

Lee, trying to keep an eye on Duncan's rear wheel, was oblivious now to what was going on anywhere else in the race. As he went banshee-ing round another sharply rising curve into a thickly wooded zone he calculated that his best chance of catching Duncan would be on the straight at the very top of the course where both the starting and finishing points were located. Moreover, that was where the biggest crowds would be and Lee relished the thought of having a good audience at the moment he went into the lead. But it wasn't going to happen on this first lap. The Scot was still too far in front for that. Lee silently urged himself on to greater effort. By now he had total faith in the performance of his machine. It had all the reliability and power he needed. So everything now depended on his own skills and determination – plus, perhaps, a little bit of luck.

To many spectators, it seemed that the only questions to be answered were *a*) which of the first two at present would be the winner; and *b*) which of the next pair would finish third. The rest seemed out of it already. But then, suddenly, dramatically, the race was thrown wide open again.

Towards the back of the pack two club-mates

who had been fighting out a personal duel went for the same narrow gap simultaneously. The collision was as violent as it was inevitable. As the bikes bounced away from each other, toppling over as they did so, they mowed down other riders like scythes.

The calamity occurred on a downhill stretch that was just tightening into a severe turn. Spectators were gathered there in strength. Instinctively, several people leapt on to the track to tend the injured and drag the fallen bikes out of the way. Seconds later, just as a yellow flag was being raised to indicate trouble, Duncan McGlew was tearing down to the same spot. His record speed that had almost enabled him to lap some of his rivals was now the cause of his own disaster.

Desperately The Flying Scot tried to brake and slide his machine round the first obstacle. But his grass track skills were no help to him in that minefield of bikes and bodies. Duncan crunched over a horizontal front wheel and pitched head first into a bush. For him, the race was over.

Lee, who'd been barely a couple of lengths adrift of the leader, glimpsed a white flag bearing a red cross. As his brain recorded that medical aid was needed for someone he tried to jink his machine between the scattering people and the litter of bikes and equipment. His strength and ability to weave at speed very nearly enabled him to get through

unscathed. But just as he attempted a gear change on the acute, rising corner, his front wheel struck an abandoned helmet; he tried to twist away but the manoeuvre caused the bike to fall over sideways. Lee just managed to get his left leg free of the frame as it came down; so he landed on his stern. In the drama of the moment he didn't even feel the pain of the bump. His only concern was that his engine should be all right.

With both leaders on the deck Nathan Pike seized his heaven-sent opportunity. Sensibly he'd slowed down on seeing the carnage ahead of him and was prepared to pick his way through it to freedom. Graham Relton, not used at all to being behind at this stage of a race, shot past Nat as he slowed down. And Graham duly paid the penalty he deserved to pay for such impetuousness. A boy who was stumbling off the track crossed his path, Graham swerved, couldn't correct in time – and slid sideways into the bush that had already claimed Duncan McGlew.

That was the moment when the race might have been called off – but, fortunately for the eventual winner, no official took that decision to hoist a red flag.

In addition to Nat, two other riders managed to improve their positions to great effect. But while Darren Parnaby threaded himself and his machine through the middle of the disaster area with commendable care Greg Shearsmith zoomed off round the perimeter and didn't even notice that he'd tangled with a marker tape at one point. Both Daz and Greg then went off in pursuit of the clear leader, Nathan Pike.

Lee, meanwhile, was reunited with his bike. To his delight, it seemed to be in perfect shape and the engine was still running sweetly. He wasn't even aware of his own bruises. A lot of ground had been lost but at least he was still in the race – and there weren't many of the starters who could say that.

Thankfully, he chased after his brother and Greg and the new, outright leader, Nathan Pike.

In spite of having been on the floor, Lee was still a long way ahead of those of the rest of the field who'd missed the great pile-up. So the race really concerned only the four riders now strung out in Indian file. Nathan believed that as long as he took no unwise risks he would keep the lead until the end; his chief worry had been the skill and flair of Lee Parnaby, the rider for whom he had the greatest respect. Nat hadn't expected Duncan to stay on two wheels on such a course and he was right. He was sure the greatest challenge would come from Lee – and now he had seen Lee, too, tumble into oblivion.

Greg, currently in third place, was determined to get the better of Darren, who was only just ahead of him. Patience had never been one of his qualities

and throughout the next lap he tried everything he knew to overtake. He was prepared to ride to the limit to win that winged trophy. But he wasn't aware that fate had already dealt him a fatal blow. For when he took an outside route round the disaster zone the tape he'd crossed had snapped and a length of it had wrapped itself around his rear brake mechanism. So, continuously, it was pulling on the brake. Even Greg's abundant strength wasn't able to cope with that problem as he tried to conjure more power from his engine. He was beginning to feel exhausted and he assumed his old head injury was taking its toll of him.

On the next downhill section Greg made a last, superhuman effort to bury Daz, as he thought of the tactic. The still gleaming Shearsmith Special soared from a ramp alongside the startled Darren; it seemed certain to overtake him but the split-second the rear wheel touched down the Special's brake locked immovably. There was a violent swerve and Greg was flung bodily across the track as the bike plunged end over end, and very spectacularly, into the banking.

Daz could hardly believe his luck. *Everything* was working out in his favour. And, because he was thinking that, his concentration wavered at just the wrong moment. On the next downhill jump which followed immediately, he failed to keep his weight at the back. Thus, on landing, the handle-bars seemed to rise up into his chest with the force of a hammer blow. Darren was badly winded. For the next hundred metres or so he thought he'd never get his breath back. In one sense he didn't, because in struggling to breathe properly he lost control of his machine.

Quite gently, he slid from the machine to the track. Fortunately he'd given up at the very spot where Uncle Ken was stationed; and within moments Mr Wragby himself had removed his elder nephew from the place of danger.

Almost before Daz was clear of the track Lee was zooming past the same spot. Nothing could have

heartened him more than the events of the last minute or so. From fourth position he'd improved to second without any extra effort on his own part. Now he could concentrate totally on catching Nat Pike and then winning the race.

As leader, Nathan was less happy than he'd care to admit. He knew he could judge the pace better when coming from behind. A glance back on one of the hairpin turns had shown him that Lee Parnaby was his nearest pursuer; and Lee, he knew, would push him all the way. Nat sensed that if Lee were given even half a chance of overtaking then he would seize it like a greyhound catching a hare.

Lee was reducing the distance between them metre by metre. It was his technique at the downhill jumps that was giving him the advantage. Well as Nat was riding, he hadn't the flair to get away so speedily from those obstacles. All the same, Nathan refused to be rattled by anything. His nerve had been good in the past and it wasn't going to fail him now.

As they went into the last lap Nathan was still just about a length in front. Twice on that final circuit Lee tried desperately to overtake immediately after a jump. Each time Nathan, with the benefit of being able to choose the shortest route, closed the gap.

Even so, when they at last regained the finishing straight, Lee, pulling wide of his rival, managed to

109

produce a final surge of power. Together the two riders flashed past the chequered flag.

The judge himself couldn't separate them. He declared the race to be the first dead-heat he'd known in his career.

'That was tremendous, Lee, tremendous,' he said after congratulating both riders. 'And all the more amazing because you were on the floor at one stage! Didn't think it was possible for you to get up again after that, let alone ride such a finish!'

Lee had never been happier. He knew he'd never ridden a better race in his life; only bad luck had prevented him from being the outright winner.

'Well done, Nat,' he said, slapping his friend and rival on the back. 'But I'm telling you this now; next time, I'm going to have first place *all to myself*.'

A Selected List of Fiction from Mammoth

While every effort is made to keep prices low, it is sometimes necessary to increase prices at short notice. Mammoth Books reserves the right to show new retail prices on covers which may differ from those previously advertised in the text or elsewhere.

The prices shown below were correct at the time of going to press.

☐	416 13972 8	**Why the Whales Came**	Michael Morpurgo	£2.50
☐	7497 0034 3	**My Friend Walter**	Michael Morpurgo	£2.50
☐	7497 0035 1	**The Animals of Farthing Wood**	Colin Dann	£2.99
☐	7497 0136 6	**I Am David**	Anne Holm	£2.50
☐	7497 0139 0	**Snow Spider**	Jenny Nimmo	£2.50
☐	7497 0140 4	**Emlyn's Moon**	Jenny Nimmo	£2.25
☐	7497 0344 X	**The Haunting**	Margaret Mahy	£2.25
☐	416 96850 3	**Catalogue of the Universe**	Margaret Mahy	£1.95
☐	7497 0051 3	**My Friend Flicka**	Mary O'Hara	£2.99
☐	7497 0079 3	**Thunderhead**	Mary O'Hara	£2.99
☐	7497 0219 2	**Green Grass of Wyoming**	Mary O'Hara	£2.99
☐	416 13722 9	**Rival Games**	Michael Hardcastle	£1.99
☐	416 13212 X	**Mascot**	Michael Hardcastle	£1.99
☐	7497 0126 9	**Half a Team**	Michael Hardcastle	£1.99
☐	416 08812 0	**The Whipping Boy**	Sid Fleischman	£1.99
☐	7497 0033 5	**The Lives of Christopher Chant**	Diana Wynne-Jones	£2.50
☐	7497 0164 1	**A Visit to Folly Castle**	Nina Beachcroft	£2.25

All these books are available at your bookshop or newsagent, or can be ordered direct from the publisher. Just tick the titles you want and fill in the form below.

Mandarin Paperbacks, Cash Sales Department, PO Box 11, Falmouth, Cornwall TR10 9EN.

Please send cheque or postal order, no currency, for purchase price quoted and allow the following for postage and packing:

UK   80p for the first book, 20p for each additional book ordered to a maximum charge of £2.00.

BFPO   80p for the first book, 20p for each additional book.

Overseas   £1.50 for the first book, £1.00 for the second and 30p for each additional book including Eire   thereafter.

NAME (Block letters) ....

ADDRESS ....

....

....